Madame Chartreuse Sweet 66's

20 cigarettes of Oriental Tobacco,
equal parts opium, papaya, and human soul.

J.P.H Vargas

i

Socrates Publishing and Media

Middletown and Hartford Connecticut

Trade Paperback

1st printing 2021

ISBN: 978-0-578-95501-8

Typesetting: Jean-Pierre Hugo Vargas

Editor: Jean-Pierre Hugo Vargas

Cover concept and sketches: Jean-Pierre Hugo Vargas

Cover illustrated: Elena Tarsius, Barcelona, Spain.

Dedicatory

To the Deists, Catholics, Muslims, Jews, Christians, Pagans, Denominations of Faiths Unknown—those who read the wisdom in the East, the old Mystics, Magicians, Norse, and those who believe in the passing of celestial bodies and worship the galaxies and ether—all women and all men of colors as varied as the Pantone hues of Earth; those of every political ideology and thought, let us all rise above, and let us build an everlasting peace. The bonds we share are as multiple as the grains of soil and sand that we all must become, we are of the same marrow, of the same passions, and overwhelming love and grace. We are incredibly powerful when indivisible, and frighteningly strong and brave when joined by our humanity.

J.P.H. Vargas Blanco

To Hugo "La Foca" Vargas

A man who dealt in the most crystalline and purest of honesty; whose autodidactic genius safely brought human beings into the vastness and starry depths of space; who could be counted on by people of science and power—dealt with kings and paupers as equals—and never lost his common touch.

Defend unto death the written word; what must be learned anew, and what must be unlearned—the wisdom of justly uttering your truth—and the bravery of love.

Overture

The seating of the audience

Prelude
Captain Inoue and Mr. Thomas R. Congress

Long ago, while crossing the vastness of the Pacific Ocean, laying telegraph cables between San Francisco and Tokyo in 1906, a year after the Russo-Japanese war ended—amidst an incredible typhoon and in danger of sinking—the Japanese steamer the Sun Maru dredged up a strange box. The sailors thought it was a marvelously novel lobster trap; we know now it was a plastic milk crate. Inside were a few odds and ends, a blue and gold box marked "Westinghouse," a folding knife, a ball of taught rubber strings, and a small chalkboard with the curious tale of a man called the "Tigermother" written in incredibly small Latin and Greek letters. The writing was imperceptible as any type of language unless viewed through a strong convex lens or high-powered astronomical telescope.

The captain of the ship wrote in his journal that the container was found "inexpressibly and unimaginably, 65 nautical miles from the next sunset, and 136 nautical miles from yesterday's dawn, between April 7th and April 9th, a few days before midnight."

When the captain arrived at his small home, nestled between a train station and a bathhouse, he retired from his two years in the merchant marines—a job given to him for his bravery in the war—and dedicated his remaining life to the translation of the chalkboard—which he discovered was a strange mix of dead, modern, contemporary, and pidgin languages—at the expense of his family and loved ones. He lived for thirty years locked in a small 7 by 13-foot study immersed in the tale of Tigermother. He learned great magic and wisdom from it. It is said that the captain gained enlightenment. In his seclusion, he was able to reach the center of the universe whilst never having left his study. Legend states that in 1952, he took a small sloop—that he traded his property for—and set sail into the earliest of dark and horrid dawns, full cry in the moonlight[1]—on a burgeoning morning as grey and loathsome as the one his father had died on— rolled into and through towering black waves—rain beat him down with the heaviest of drops—screaming with violent passion and gripping the rudder with the thickly calloused hands of a shipmaster; and as the sails flapped thunderously, whipping and beating the wind like koto drums; memories of his valiant comrades firing off 8-inch guns into the Russian

---

[1] . "Full cry in the moonlight" taken directly from Sir Arthur Conan Doyle's *The Hound of the Baskervilles*. Dr. Mortimer (MRCS) reads the cautionary tale as laid down by Hugo Baskerville to his sons. Sherlock Holmes notes aloud the use of archaic and outdated language.

fleet, and their ghoulish moans; their cries and gasps when enemy shells burst over their bow and stern entered his heart; those things he had kept hidden away came back to him. He saw his comrade Lt. Ochiai, a good and treasured friend in his mind's eye; stoically holding his torn belly together, barking orders to the midshipmen "Ute!," "Ute!," as he slowly bled to death, standing, fighting, on the deck of their old warship. The captain ripped the ropes holding the sails, with the bottomless anger and passion he felt the day his wife left him for another, licked his lips in anticipation of what adventures were to come, and from the bottom of his nut-brown barrel chest, from the depth of his brave Japanese guts—his "Hara,"—he let out the fiercest "Banzai" ever loosed by any warrior, and disappeared into the eye of a typhoon, never to be seen again.

The following poems were found written in English upon various bits of paper that covered the walls of his claustrophobic study. The letter that follows Inoue's poem was found undated and with an undeliverable return address, written on thick paper of South American manufacture without watermark; it had been pinned to a board folded in half.[2]

---

[2] This passage was inspired from a personal memory months after an examination of the novel "The Sign of the Four," by Sir Arthur Conan Doyle. The language expressed in the dialog of the novel—when Mary Morstan hands over an impressively unique letter to Mr. Holmes—was the basis for the altered phrase in this novel. It was during a carriage ride to visit Pondicherry Lodge in Upper Norwood at the request of Thaddeus Sholto.

Testament and Oath of Captain Sota Inoue

I, Sota Inoue, captain of the Sun Maru, sailor and valiant
mariner who fought the Russian fleet, adventurer, and
autodidact who is now learned with all wisdom, go to search
for the Tigermother, out in the fortunate islands, the isles of
the blessed, illuminated below by the quill pen of J.R. Lowell,[3]
who may have seen or heard of that place, or somehow met
those few privileged to visit the isles:

. . . .

"Whatever of true life there was in thee,
Leaps in our age's veins;
Weird still they bent and wrinkled empery,
And shake thine idle chains; —
To thee thy dross is clinging,
For us thy martyrs die, thy prophets see,
Thy poets still are singing.
Here, 'mid the bleak waves of our strife and care,
Float the green Fortunate Isles,
Where all the hero-spirits dwell and share
Our martyrdoms and toils.

. . . .

The present moves attended
With all of brave and excellence and fair
That made the old time splendid.[4]"

---

[3] The author is drawn greatly to the work of Lowell in the field of linguistics.
In the late 1800's, Lowell began to use "New England Vernacular," or the
"Common Language of the New England People" in his prose. The author
believes that language itself can never be quantified in any measure, or fully
cataloged in any corpora linguistica in its entire wholeness. The fluidity and
evolution of language moves at a pace whose rapidity makes codification "for
ongoing time" impossible. Databases can be maintained, but an analysis of
such lexical information would be subjective, since 1 human, or a group, or
chain, of humans, cannot live long enough to ever find the 'end' of a language
itself, from its origins. This has all been noted before the time of Lowell,
however, since the author chose these stanzas to elucidate expressive schema
in this work, he thought it prudent to use Lowell for this example on language
and its evolution.
[4] . J.R. Lowell, "To the Past." Stanzas VIII and IX

I, Sota Inoue, will go on until dawn stops breaking and the morning sun stops rising, into the blue ocean, over waves and through waters as deep as the human heart to dialog with gods. I leave you all with the words of Milton, who alludes to the islands far off into the western ocean, and with the letter I transcribed over years of solitude, longing, and loathing, written by my unknown friend, the Tigermother.

....

"Like those Hesperian gardens famed of old,
Fortunate fields and groves and flowery vales,
Thrice happy isles."[5]

....

-Captain Sota-

First Letter of Matanza
Smaller print

"The Tigermother"
Address not registered
Wavemaker and Rainmaker
Laid to rest
In the Eastern or Western Ocean

Homo Sapiens
Local Group: "Orion Arm"
$2/3^{rd}$ right of the Center
Galaxy: "Milky Way"
3rd interstellar body orbiting "Sol"

Peoples of all shapes and colors, ideas, beliefs, are constructed by their multitude complexities and ignorance. I was as well. I would be a static character in a novel, if I were to be written about, that is. I feel as though I am not changing, as though I only observe what is happening in bracing and cold indifference. I am a student of the

---

[5] . *Paradise Lost*, Book III, 168.

absurd here. I have heard tell that to compose a tale of magic and lore, there must be some end to a journey, helpers, and friends; but I have none here, nor can I feel. Nothing passes through my heart and its occasional off-tempo beat except the want to not engage with anything that could matter, material or immaterial. In every sense, I am as I should be, one who only observes and listens, occasionally entering the narrative with some form, some idea or conflict, yet, bubbling violently under the mired and complex wholeness of my "being, or soul," whatever entire breadth and scope I believe I am— an animal of reason and ambiguous prose—is just the passionately suffered wish to have an important and good friend.

There is no climax or story to be found inside these pages—no wisdom—as my time on these beaches is spent looking for ideas entertaining the absolute nothingness that passes through all our minds daily; daydreams and anxieties; rabbit hole irrational thoughts; and philosophies that others have thought up and we unknowingly credit to ourselves. If I could do this all over, I would dedicate myself to a long and challenging course of readings that could serve me as a portal into the learned world, so one day, if I applied myself, and my experiences, I could come up with some form of original thought, something *mine*. But to do so would require analytical and synoptical study of an immense scale that would take decades. But now here, I have the time, yet lack the literature.

Time doesn't apply to these islands, of which next to nothing is known, since the only account we have of them are in the legends of the old peoples, the Ancient Greeks, Romans, and Phoenicians; however, they do exist, impermeable to the forces surrounding them, as if encased and bound inside an eggshell and still yet enveloped in unending space: they exist immune to time. That strange feeling one gets on a dangerous brush with death, or after a very still and broken heart that ceases to beat for a lover, those feelings are the islands calling you. Now, each person has their own circumstances that lead them to the outer islands far in the western ocean. Each stay on these lands is different for everyone who visits them, some stay longer than others; some have been here since the beginning, since the fires of peoples, tribes, and gods, were first lit.

So, if one reads this letter, find me and be my friend, come talk and tell stories, and sit with me as an equal, for here at least we are all composed of the same matter, the matter of fear and complications, the residue of loss and the occasional memory of happiness—the meat has been torn off our bones, and we all now exist as the excommunicated few.

Sincerely,

Señor Matanza

* *The chalkboard, with the tale marked up in different colored chalk upon it, was taken to Japan's Ministry of Defense and had been worked on continuously in secret until a few years ago, when it came into my possession, (Mr. Thomas R. Congress), through the shadiest and most unethical dealings I've ever had to agree with; as payment for helping clear up a blackmail case involving the future heir of a Japanese automobile mogul, and the top brass in the Japanese Self-Defense Forces research division. I have finished the work started in good captain Inuoe's name; set it down as gospel; motivated only by strong whisky highballs, loneliness, traipses with danger; the foulest of people, and infinitely graced by godless moral deviancy.* *

"Addendum to the file"

This entire account, and the books that follow, were found written inside of three leather-covered moleskin journals belonging to Mr. Thomas R. Congress MSc, dated October 19th 1981, Hartford CT, on the occasion of his death, May 16th 1999, where, during his funeral, those very few that attended played "Desperados Under the Eaves" by Warren Zevon, marveled at what a beautiful and sunny day it was, until, most curiously, at 10:04am, were collectively shocked by the most impossible and epic downpour ever recorded in New England history; during the driest and brightest day notated by all mankind. As the sky let loose and shook the old church's ribs; the stations of the cross started to crumble, the faltering spires shook and dented the bell, and the cathedral chandeliers dropped bits of jeweled glass onto the floor and pews; the priest hurriedly signed the cross with his left hand against his chest, ripped off his wooden rosary beads—tearing open his frock—shattered them violently against the marble chapel floor, and exclaimed thunderously to the four congregants attending the service— with bubbled spittle and thick rabid foam at the corners of his chapped mouth—"The devil is getting married today! God damn you! God damn all you rats!" He collapsed behind the altar into a gelatinous and tonic-clonic, grand-mal mess.

A sharply dressed man, in a royal blue three-piece suit, leaned carelessly against the back pillar of the chapel, unfazed; visibly elated and grinning at this grotesque preamble to Mr. Congress' new after-life. He inserted a cassette of Mozart's adagio and fugue in C minor into a battery powered boom box, pressed play, and derisively laughed at the spectacle of the broken holy man. The booming music echoed in the shaking and shivering cathedral. The double bass in the second movement of Mozart's piece blew out both 10-inch speakers and cracked the baptismal fountain. He lit a cigarette with a Swedish three-star match; burned his index finger with a crisp sizzle as he extinguished the flame. He dipped his hand into the leaking basin of holy water to relieve the sting. The man took two thick drags of the tobacco, flicked the still burning cigarette onto the marble floor, and with the grace of a bediamonded and urbane ballet dancer, he silently sauntered and slid out of the church. He slammed the creaky and heavy oaken doors with such thunderous force that the brass Latin cross handles were torn off; struck the granite steps—chimed harmoniously in tempo with the heaving bell in the tower—and punctuated the lurching of the church's innards and rumbling breath like the mellifluous wheezes of struggled gulps of air made by dying man in his final throes. The building was choking. The priest was choking. Nobody in pews of the church batted an eye. Nobody was surprised.

Aria

La Siesta del duende San Lazaro

St Lazarus and his love of lies

1

I was dreaming of the sand from the beach on their feet. I was dreaming I was pulling the sand grain by grain from each one of their toes. I was dreaming they had their knees bolted together and their feet apart. Their body smelled of brine. I dreamt they were looking away as I put their socks on and kissed their knees. My hair had been knotted and curled by the salt water. Theirs still dripped like blond and amber brushstrokes. I thought I saw them once in a painting by Gauguin. I thought I saw their soul at least. They may have been the muse that sent Van Gogh into oblivion. Or maybe they were just pure light and color, like Matisse's last sheets of colored paper thrown onto the floor from his deathbed. I think about them at length on some occasions as I sleep. I can think when I sleep. Other times they just appear as random fragments, floating and collecting towards their own center, like in the eye of a dying hurricane, or the cone of a whirlpool. They glimmer, irradiated, as if immured by constellations, and

13

hanging loosely, easily in the dark dawn, floating, as if gently cupped in Orion's outstretched hand.

Dreams come as they do, every night to collect on my sins and regrets. They keep me accountable. That is why I am here, to remember and to be broken of my ethereal bond by the cacophony that is him, the ocean master. Clad in burlap, and wearing wooden flip-flops, he will slap me out of my glorious rhapsody and into repetitious conversation that revolves around the absurd, hoping to teach me the ways around the glory of heaven while disregarding any notion of God. Plotting the takeover of the fishmonger's stands, stealing and cheating. Did I come here? I may have. I may have been drugged, most likely, since I have no recollection of arriving here, but I must have come on my own. I brought my toothbrush. I think I came here to learn from him, the seer of the sea, this incubus, to learn how to become evil.

"Wake up!" he screamed; a decibel short of snapping a vocal cord. I vaulted off the sandy mat that held my dreaming mind off the floor, fingered, poked, and prodded the vacuous expanses of surface area that consisted of a few shelves, containing pink, purple, green, blue, and red glass bottles, all of which were filled with formaldehyde and contained the remains of various sea creatures he thought were beautiful. The black bottle in the corner contained the soul of the fishmonger's wife. He told me he stole it from her as she was sleeping under a palm tree with a half-eaten papaya in her hand. At last, my pinky found where I had placed my oversized spectacles. These spectacles were by no means ordinary. Constructed out of thick heavy black plastic, and with lenses as large as the bottom of a bottle of cheap rum; but

I could see everything. He told me he would teach me to look inside a man's greatest fear, or to see what a woman desired most. He had not taught me any tricks yet, for now the ridiculousness of the mammoth spectacles burdened me— without them I was blind, like the tiny cave shrimp that make their life deep within the cavernous interior of the fishmonger's rock holes. I checked to see if my heart was beating. It was not.

"You woke me out of my dream," I said as I adjusted the spectacles carefully onto my nose, making sure to do it slowly as the weight alone could easily snap a child's neck.

"You needed to be arisen, my dear Señor Matanza, mother of tigers. You cry for them in your sleep. I could hear the pitter patter of your tears wetting your straw mat, making the grains of sand on my floor stick to each other. That I will not allow." He, the man who has enveloped me into a continuity of cyclical and tornado-like conversations, the man who has broken his covenant with his soul at the deepest and darkest edge of the world, the only man who can laugh in the face of the glory of the most high, is the most revered and unholy St. Lazarus, according to him, famous in certain circles of influence, although I would, by judging his tiny home, ramshackle living arrangements, and strangeness, see his prolific résumé as a bit of a stretch.

He stood before me dressed in a shirt he had made from a burlap sack and old flour bags, with fitted sleeves and pieces of broken coral for buttons. His shorts went a little bit lower than his boney knees, which looked like the sun-beaten elbows of a mummified man. His flip-flops were made of solid palm wood, and the strap between his toes and the wrapping that covered the rest of his toe knuckles were made of palm-fronds that had been carefully separated and woven together with the greatest care, almost matching the level of quality you would see in the great silk makers of the opium world. I fixed my glasses tight on the bridge of my nose and looked at him, my eyeballs must have looked four times the size as seen through the lenses, and every time I blinked, my magnified brown eyelashes probably looked as if they caught the ocean breeze and tried to fly off my face.

"I see nothing, nothing but you looking at me."

He paused for a moment and smiled, showing his engorged bloody gums and stained teeth. "Can you see me?" St. Lazarus asked as he breathed in deeply and expanded his chest, hopping and squatting, curling his arm around his head and picking at his hair, while scratching his left armpit with the long phalanges of his left hand. He finished by howling and baring his canine teeth, beating at his chest with the ferocity of a silverback gorilla.

"I see a man telling a lie right now," I said as I looked over his weather-beaten, leathery face, with deep folded creases and wrinkles as if soft and velvety smooth suede had been dried in the aridity and heat of a furnace—his years in the ocean showed.

"Why do you think I lie to you right now, Señor Matanza?" He arched his lean, sinuous, dark-skinned body forward and managed to reach mine. He placed his forehead onto mine and blew smoke in my face. He had been hiding a burning cigarette in his mouth this whole time.

"I'm calling you a liar because you are acting like a monkey. You are not a monkey, although by your untidy habits and ape-like dexterity I wouldn't be surprised if by chance you have some type of baboon guts, or monkey blood flowing through your garden hose veins. Barring the exceptional experience of you one day in the future launching a turd through the air with your bare hands, which I hope never happens, I conclude upon your current actions that you are not a monkey, so I say that you are lying." St. Lazarus ran his obscenely long fingers through his white, yellowing, nappy, salt-crusted hair, and, laughing a low chuckle like the engine of a Chevy truck revving up and popping exhaust and uttering bangs, he wheezed quite a bit and choked out a few garbled words while his shallow green eyes darted back and forth across the room, mapping and calculating, curving his references, and slowly organizing a response. Besides being the man about town, prison keeper, holy man, God to himself, disheveled, disorganized, and oblivious, all at the same time, he responded to every query with an intense analytical level of function. It may take him days of beard and hair stroking, eyes darting from horizon to shadows, the click of his slick flip-flops, that is how I could keep him busy. Conversation was his broken rib. Conversation was his Eve.

St. Lazarus took a large breath, his languid dark face bursting open like a dying orchid. He raised his arms and spread his fingers almost over the entirety of the inside of the palm hut. "Apollo!" he shouted. "Ceyx and Halcyone!" he bellowed louder as he entered more into thought. "Cadmus! Minerva! Daedalus!" He began breathing himself into hyperventilation. The names kept coming, faster and faster. I could see them bounce off the walls and knock over bottles of rum and some chipped the dried mud from the hearth. Some names came out with such force that they put a hole right through the wall of the palm-frond hut. He was verbose with the nomenclature, one name at a time, but the names shot out fast. He was spouting them out like a choking garden hose right before the deluge of cold water, and they resounded like the rat-a-tat-tat of pops, bangs, and cartridge casings bouncing off the floor when a Kalashnikov is being fired into an empty room. The name "Ariadne" nearly knocked me out. Now, to the regular observer seeing language is impossible, but when St. Lazarus becomes verbose to prove a point, and one is wearing absurd forty-five-pound spectacles that are becoming quite unctuous at the bridge of one's nose and slipping off one's face, well, then one can see pretty much anything one wishes.

Not being one to stay for the rest of his outbursts, I slowly moved for the door. I had not seen the sun in months; only small icicles of light managed to break the seams of the palm-frond hut, illuminating and dividing the floor into little bars of yellow light, and making the bottles shiny and pretty like a vision from an abstract nighttime sky. St. Lazarus was settling down and I pushed him aside for the door. As I walked out, I could see God, the sun. I could envision the chariot of Helios dragging it over the blue and white sky. I felt the light burn me, all the beautifully carcinogenic rays bearing upon my amber skin. I listened hard to the sand. It crackled like stepping on fresh snow that had a layer of thin ice from a winter rainfall, and I could hear and feel the friction on each tiny granule of eroded stone that became compressed against the bottom of my foot. "St. Lazarus!" I shouted at the top of my lungs. He did not hear me. He was still working out why I'd called his actions lies. "St. Lazarus!" I shouted even louder. "Why didn't you ever let me out of the hut? This place is hot and marvelous!" I heard nothing. Then I began to hear a faint chuckle. As if from far away it grew nearer, and nearer, and nearer, and then, as if carried by a sonic boom, it was upon me.

"You were dreaming, Señor Matanza. I am not the kind of man who would disturb you as you dreamt about whatever it is that you dream about." I stared at St. Lazarus' pitifully disheveled appearance. I could smell him he was so close. He was musky like ambergris and rum; it was an earthy umami smell like spoiled milk, chives; the air around his mouth tasted of rancid butter. "Ah, I say you were dreaming of the one, the creator, our mother-father, and only when you dream do you remember things, places, people. With time it will come, the memories of your sufferings; but now it's time for the inscrutable and mysterious Señor Matanza to wake and do my daily business. Only a few simple tasks are all I ask, nothing more, nothing less." Having never been out of the hut, I wondered for a moment what kind of things surrounded us, and what kind of business St. Lazarus engaged in. From a practical standpoint, I would stay and do the best I could to help with his tasks, for I didn't know where I was or for that matter, anything about this place.

"St. Lazarus, listen," I said. "Tell me about your business when the moment is right. There is a time for everything, and it seems as though I will be going nowhere in particular for quite a while, here with you, in this place. Tell me about my dreams, I wish to know about them, about what I was, and who I was." There was an unease I felt there, and I didn't understand the magic of that place, or what I was. There was no amnesia, nothing barring me form learning, and slowly every night I pieced together a bit of what I was, if I was anything at all.

"Ah, the sun goes up and down, it rises in the west and sets in the east, it marks our time here. You sleep when the sun goes down, and hopefully you see our mother-father when you sleep. What you learn is up to you. If you so choose not to, then don't be troubled. This is what is real for you, what happened before is in the land of myths and legends." St. Lazarus, if human, was odd, and, if anything other than human, was odd still, regardless of what reality I was composed in, at that moment, and even if my safety was in jeopardy, or if an adventure or tragedy was soon evident; I would have to be patient. St. Lazarus sat down on the sand, crossed his cartoonishly long and sunburned legs; stuck his forefinger into the pocket of his cheek and let out a loud pop, lit a "Madame Chartreuse Sweet 66" cigarette, took an inhale so long that he consumed the tobacco in one go, and began to explain the word he found that proved that acting like a gorilla is not a lie. "Expression."

St. Lazarus looked down at me since he measured an—almost—incalculable seven feet tall. Although sometimes he would seem smaller. Not that he had the ability to change size; his fictitious and fluctuating personality affected his unreasonable changes in size. Sometimes he resembled a new and crisp, shiny, vacuum-produced plastic figurine; other times, he resembled strands of taut rubber tied together, a wobbly and fluid, dark, intriguing man ransacked by grog.

"I did not lie in acting like a monkey. It is you who lied, Señor Matanza. Your thoughts betrayed you. Expression from mind to body can never lie. It can only heighten what is real. Artists, either good or bad people, make things that bring a pinnacle of what others do not see, they punctuate our lies and feelings." St. Lazarus smiled, his dark yellow teeth shining a dull greenish brown, like giant kernels of rotten corn.

"My thoughts of you do not make me a liar, St. Lazarus. You were acting as something you are not. Therefore, as innocent as acting may be, I will state that all actors and artists are liars." I struggled to keep my head raised to look into the liver-colored whites of his loopy eyeballs.

"Yes, yes, my chum, my pal, my olive-skinned Matanza! You may state what you wish, but you keep in your tiny little head this idea. I played a monkey. I made art. To create what is false, an expression, a rule must bend for me, for I am no monkey in this world, and in this world the monkey I played is not, he is an imitation, like me, like you, Matanza. We exist far away. In what is real." I looked at St. Lazarus' nappy white hair, turning yellow at the ends. He made some sense, I suppose. Could art be an imitation? The thought of me not existing was troubling, for if I do not exist in the real[6] then what am I to this place? A specter, a vision, a collection of misplaced memories, nightmares, fears, anxieties, and abnormalities? As I sat and unraveled the intricate and delicate meat of what this disparaging reprobate had just spilled onto my lap, the thought of St. Lazarus being a wise man began to enter my head. I had been here for what seemed months and yet I slept, thought, and heard him in my dreams. Only now had I ventured outside and been able to breathe in some of our

---

[6] . In the "Platonic" method of thought.

shared creation. Only now in ridiculous ciphers and anesthetizing prose had he begun to talk to me. St. Lazarus jumped straight up onto a fallen palm tree and began to balance himself on his tiptoes, then bent his back into a crescent and touched the sand with his fingertips.

The sun was blinding white. It was hot. I was shirtless, and my tan cargo shorts were wet. Sweat was dripping down my chest and pooling in my belly button. "You should go now and take a look around yourself, see what you see," St. Lazarus advised. "You have been dreaming about the one truth, her/him for too long. See where you are now." I raised my head since the ridiculous pair of glasses were beginning to weigh more and more and I looked out. I saw a palm tree, tall and thick. Its brother tree must have fallen, and now St. Lazarus stood upon him. I saw sand as white, peach, and cream colored, pink in some parts like the skin on the headiest and most innocuous body parts of loose women I'd laid with. The sun was not in the blue sky. There shone only a bright light everywhere. My shadow turned with me. This was a place where shadows had power. I turned to my back to see what lay behind. The small palm hut stood bare. There was a fire pit I'd failed to see when I left the room earlier, empty bottles of rum laid among enormous fishbones. The fishbones of demon creatures that must reside in the deepest part of the ocean, where only the careless enter, with knife in hand, and net, to drag a monstrosity, Neptune's unholy creations, onto land, or die. The hut was made between two bent palm trees. It looked larger from the inside. Behind the hut I could see black rough, porous volcanic rocks, as jagged as they were intimidating, probably the only place Hephaestus made the mistake of dropping a handful of ash. The only way through this mess of crags and boulders was a narrow and smoothed-out path carved from St. Lazarus' eternity of walking the same route to the fishmonger's home. I saw nothing else. I squinted but I could not see a horizon in any direction. In my confusion I only saw space and the area before me. I was seeing what the glasses were letting me see.

"You will only see what I will you to see," St Lazarus said as he jumped of the palm log, noticing my squinting. He resembled a goliath frog as his legs sprang him into the air, his hands reached for the blue sky, and he landed on all fours, having successfully cleared the giant fishbones and the fire pit. "You are not ready to see this place. First you must converse with me, and converse again, and with others, and then we shall see where your true argument lies, Señor Matanza. Then I will teach you to hunt the big fish, and to drink rum well, and to fornicate with the sea when the moon is full and the tide is out. For now, I will limit you—for your own safety, of course— you will see what I want you to see. Then you will sleep, then you will dream. After which you will be able to see what *you* want."

I began thinking that this was folly, a game, and I began to understand the rules St. Lazarus had in his game theory. Was it the clear definition of the bottom of the seven liberal arts: trivium? I couldn't be sure, but logic, theory, conversation, rules of the spoken tradition, reasoning, the whispers spoken about me during parties, drunken word games, passing notes during class, everything that is communication, was massed together and thrown into the air by the whipping wind that was St. Lazarus, like the breeze playing with dead leaves in the autumn and arranging them back into place and setting them down in my mind.

The rules were simple. I had to converse, and converse again. That equals two conversations. I knew a simple dialog wouldn't suffice; therefore, I would have to prepare myself for the inevitable conundrum that would arise when a being of unusual and somewhat precarious tendencies, like St. Lazarus, was to plant a deep query—be it based in my reality or in his strange fallacies and revolving logic. "St. Lazarus!" I yelled. He was lying on his back on the sand, wearing a palm-frond hat to cover his eyes. He rolled to one side, and then to the other, like a turtle getting off its back. He seemed to be ignoring me. "Your holiness," I said mockingly. "Please do me the favor of getting up and sitting straight as a board; have a conversation with me." St. Lazarus croaked out a throaty chuckle, rubbed his tight cannonball gut, sighed a finicky feline purr, sat up and crossed his legs, intertwining his size twenty-five feet into his thighs, reached into the pocket of his burlap shirt, and pulled out the ass end of a chewed-up cigar.

"You want to talk now, man-child?" he said as he slowly bit into the cigar, then jolted for an instant and quickly thrust his head into the fire pit to light it. He inhaled deeply. I could hear the skin on his chest stretch like old vinyl on a used junkyard car seat as his torso expanded. His exhale sounded like the bellows and creaks of a steam ship crossing the Atlantic and was as toxic as a yellow fog pea soup day in Victorian London. "You will talk now, we shall talk. If you move me and you are nothing but purely selfish, you will see more, and you will live a better life." St. Lazarus got up off the ground and began to walk towards the hut. He stepped over the fire pit and crushed fishbones as thick as my arm with the bottom of his flip-flops. "You, Señor Matanza, you wait, sit and wait. We will talk." He disappeared into the palm-frond hut. I was left to my own devices. I tried to remember my dreams, and that thing, that person I speak with, whatever it may be, male, female—friend or foe—but it would only come to me in sleep. If it was a woman, I wished to taste her, to sink into her, melt myself into her soft body, pass a night as a cricket at her bedside, to be the moan of pleasure, the rapture she desires—poetically speaking of course—just to give my fantasies some grace instead of the true vileness and deviant perversity that really crossed my mind. There seemed to be a lack of females here. However, if it was a man, I would hope him to be a normal influence on me, since his holiness St. Lazarus seemed comfortable with lies and lechery and had a disdain for any kind of interaction that didn't border upon the absurd. However, those are all waking thoughts and wishes. Wishes do not come true, ever; they are only the conscious manifestations of the wet dreams of our ego.

St. Lazarus emerged from the palm-frond hut. He was wearing a burlap robe over his burlap shirt, carrying with him a burlap satchel filled with all sorts of bottles. He had black knitted fingerless gloves that he had stolen from the fishmonger when the fishmonger was sick from eating too much honeydew melon. On top of his head he had placed a hat made from riveted shiny sheets of copper. It resembled a nón lá, the Vietcong guerrilla's headpiece, except it was metal and glistened so brightly in the sunlight that reflections from it were causing some areas of dried-up dune grass to smolder and bellow smoke. The little bells that were hanging like

Chinese ornamental lights from the brim of his copper hat were ringing and dinging violently as he crouched down into a deep squat, sprang up, and leapt over the fire pit and the bones. He was as graceful as a zebra in its final death throes being pulled under the murky waters in some African country by a Nile crocodile. He took his seat in front of me on his palm tree stump and smiled while chewing on the end of the burning cigar. St. Lazarus blew three smoke rings and shot a line of pure white ash through their center, purifying the air like sage, just as Vesuvius had done to the heathens. I smiled at him. "That took some talent," I said, looking at his robe, which was more of a poncho.

"I can do many things, young Señor Matanza. We are here to talk. Not to show or make magic or entertain," said St. Lazarus as he put his hands under his poncho.

"What are we going to talk about?" I asked him, hoping that we could get this over with. "How long are we going to talk for?" I asked. He shook his head as if disapproving my inquiries.

"What we shall talk about is…" He stopped and thought for a second. "…No, what *you* will talk about is bullshit."

"Bullshit?" I asked.

"Yes, you must move me to some degree by bullshitting me."

"Bullshit about what?" I asked, annoyed.

"This," he said as he took his hands from under his poncho to reveal an earthen pot filled with dirt.

I found myself befuddled by his request to bullshit him. The only subject I had was an earthen pot filled with dirt. It would take a masterful bullshit artist indeed to bullshit a de-sanctified bastard child of the mother-father—their strange creation—this abhorrent, deviant, and deformed Prometheus; especially being such a tricky fiend as St. Lazarus was. "Is my only topic this earthen pot filled with dirt?" I asked, hoping to get a little more from him.

"No, you get one more. My chewed-up cigar." He laid the earthen pot down, raised his foot to his mouth, bending his knee in a manner that made the laws of human kinesiology and articulatory mechanics moot; he seemed composed of putty and pliable melted plastic. His knee sounded gritty, like a bag of sand being popped inside of a bucket of water. He groaned an utterance an old man would make and put the end of the cigar out with the bottom of his big toe, searing and sizzling, unfurling a dark grey smoke that smelled like burnt hair. He laid the cigar down on the sand next to the earthen pot and smiled at me—not a regular smile, but an impish smile with a wicked disposition. "If you can bullshit me with these two items, I will let you see everything and dialog with the gods; you may also go when the sun is high as long as your path is chosen. But you must return every night to dream here at the palm hut."

I sat across from the two objects, spread my legs out straight, took a short shallow breath, and slowly began to formulate an idea of how I could improvise a dialog on these two seemingly random objects. St. Lazarus sat slumped against a log with his copper hat and bells covering his eyes, his legs were apart, and he still wore that mockingly disturbing grin from ear to ear. "This is your only chance, to see, to rid yourself of those glasses," St. Lazarus said as he suddenly sprang to the balls of his feet and closed fists, on all fours, like a strong lion, a king of the pride. His demeanor changed into that of an animal. He paced around me and the fire, breathing heavy intense breaths. "Go on now, my dear Señor Matanza! You're domesticated! You are trash, rotten trash!" he roared. "Be selfish! Move me!" I tried to calm my core. I was panic stricken for a moment and felt pressed; he was a creature without boundaries. The sparks off the burning wood in the fire pit were falling like little Molotov cocktails, arching in a beautiful parabola before disintegrating into the air. The wind at my back stirred my heart to think. The smell of burning grass and wood was perfect, the wind was perfect, and my heart was coming back to me. I could feel each beat stir my veins like the rhythm of a junked-up calypso band on too much cocaine. St. Lazarus paced too close to me; a palpable wave of tension pulled the hairs up on the back of my neck. I pushed him away. "Good now, son of man, move me," he whispered into my face. I could smell the salt water and grog and fishbones on his breath. I drew the two objects into my lap, the cigar and the earthen pot. St. Lazarus burst into laughter, a loud gregarious bellow that puttered out like a popped wheezy rubber balloon. "You can't bullshit and be selfish by only holding—go on now."

I ignored him and went with the impulses of my now beating heart. I figured I might as well, since having been here it hadn't even beaten once. I am, or was, a practical man, I thought, sure I cannot be, but for this once I will tune into whatever nonsense I can improvise. I dug a small hole into the dirt in the pot and carefully placed the cigar inside. I made sure to cover all the exposed parts of the wrapped tobacco, and I placed the pot back down on the ground. St. Lazarus sat amused at my movements. He was picking and stroking his patchy gray beard. The ends of his white mustache had yellowed from strong medicine and tobacco, and he removed a bit of fish that was stuck to the bottom of his whiskers and put it into his mouth, chewing it once over and spitting it out. He had taken a seat in front of his palm log after pacing for what seemed hours. "Take your place at my table and speak lies, my good friend. Step onto your podium." I assumed he meant to stand on the rotting palm log. I brought the pot with the cigar planted inside, placed it before me on the ground, and stood up on the palm log. "You have acted, planting a cigar; now move me with selfish bullshit about your actions." I knew that now, with a beating heart and less wracked by panic, I could accomplish this task.

"I will go with what is left of my core, my heart, St. Lazarus. It came back at this moment for a reason, maybe a gorgeous and nervy arrhythmia, but it seems to be functioning at least," I said proudly as I stood before a ridiculous and illogical man, about to give a short dissertation on the nature of planting cigars.

"Ah, you must worry now, a heart is a bad thing to have here on the fortunate isles out in the fathomless western ocean where we live." St. Lazarus looked grave, serious, a look I did not expect to see in his muddy eyes. He was most likely warning me of some random danger or terrifying misadventure. "Begin your soliloquy; be as selfish as humanly possible."

I puffed out my chest, nervously coiled a brown curl hanging low on my brow from sweat, buried my toes in the sand, and began speaking. "Plant a cigar. I have always wondered—that is to say—I have conducted many studies on what would happen if I were to plant a cigar. Would Fidel Castro pop his tiny little head out of from the womb of the earth and attempt to indoctrinate me? No, absolutely not! What I can conclude, if anything, from my preliminary studies, is that the cigar would just rot away in the dirt. Just like any humanistic or political or religious ideal, or men for that matter, would rot away. Speaking of men and decay. Aren't they degenerates and apostates, men that have wasted our time and sympathy; aren't they the most treacherous enemies of humankind, liars, manipulators, writers, and teachers of the false doctrine, filling the air with noxious inveracity and disease?" I took a series of staccato breaths; my heartbeat was irregular. However, as I looked at St. Lazarus, he seemed to have a disinterested and disdainful look upon his weather-beaten face. I raised my voice, picked up the pace of my beating words, and began to improvise again. "Man was put onto this Earth to follow someone or some ideal. How then does a man—a good or a bad man—be he big or little—a philosopher or a fool—the pope or a liar—follow his own dream? The answer is simple: be selfish. I have always found myself at this same juxtaposition; behind me lay the long straight line of mediocrity, ahead a cracked and bumpy path to greatness." I breathed in deeply and saw that St. Lazarus was looking at my face as I spoke, while he chewed a sprig of dune grass and scratched his paunchy belly, playing with his belly button before sniffing his finger. My heart continued to flow, the words were being popped and snapped out of my mouth like a tight snare drum in a college marching band. I continued: "You could be a liar and remain mediocre. To be great, you must manipulate, to use and destroy people, to abuse your competition's sensibilities, and finally, to violate everything that stands in your way. There is not much separating a brigand from a successful person; all successful people deserve notoriety for all the wool they have pulled. Have I become jaded for reaching this conclusion? No, I have not. My ideas are solid and rich, established and sublime. One must learn to discard the ethereal, the impractical, and what may seem to you as smart. Embrace the perfidious, the perfunctory, and the prosperity! Remember, the more people you step on, the higher you can go."

I sat on the palm log and said nothing; it was beginning to become night and I could hear the crickets coming from the dune grass thicket that had not been set on fire by the reflections of Roscoe's copper hat. The sparks were still flying, and my heart was dying. The wind must have whipped it into a fervor for a short time. But I knew the wind was not fickle there and if it has doubled my strength, and trusted me, it may do so again. I put my hand in the soil of the earthen pot and threw some towards the dying sky. It took with it my message of penance. Hopefully the wind would whisper its forgiveness for the enormous lie I had just spoken. St. Lazarus had moved me to grind against my heart.

"Señor Matanza, why are you here? Have you thought about that?" asked St. Lazarus while swilling grog water around his mouth and spitting it out onto the ground, leaving a brown tar-like substance covering the pink sand, which oozed for a second and puddled into a thick reeking oily bubble.

"All I know is that I have been sleeping and seeing my good, trusted friend the [her/him,] whose duality makes me smile," I said as I stuck my finger into the oozing reek that St. Lazarus spat out.

"Well, you won't see them again, for that was only a part of your short journey through these islands. I will say you are here for an eternity; however you choose to pass that time is up to you." Having little to no recollection of any of my past misadventures or lives, if one believes in reincarnation, I thought that I had to come to terms with that concept of the utmost moment. "There is no particular reason for you to be here, for whatever you call this place, and whatever you deem it to be, is only for you. It is your proper burial ground." I ran my fingers across my eyes since I had some sticky mucous that itched and suppurated from the strong winds.

"Am I to think that this life is only for me?"

"Yessir," said St. Lazarus, and now that you know how to bullshit properly, and understand that lies and art are one and the same, you can start learning how to tell a story. For stories, fictions, even if based upon truths, are all lies. And the fastest way into seducing anyone, to sell them something they don't need, become friends, lovers, partners, is through an enticing tale. Since we have no books around us, you will have to learn to invent your tales, short tales, since your audience has a terrible attention span."

"Who is to be my audience?" said I, wondering at who else was here on these islands with us.

"We shall soon see, since I am one who cannot hide my curiosity during these moments."

St. Lazarus sat crossed legged upon the sand near the expiring embers, fidgeted for a brief second with a hemp cord, and pulled his bag full of small bottles towards his legs, then gestured for me to come forward. "Bring the earthen pot," he asked. I got off the rough palm log and picked up the earthen pot. Stepping onto the loose sand, I felt it flow under and over my toes. A breeze came in and stirred the embers into flames again. St. Lazarus sat legs crossed, looking into my eyes, licking his chapped lips. He had opened a bottle of boot-legged rum and poured it into two tin cans. "Rum," he said. "When a benevolent little new man, like you, full of humanity and lenity, is made to lie, a lie that can break his heart, it makes me incredibly happy, and nothing but rum can fix that. I love making you sad, and, of course, drinking heavily."

I sat down next to St. Lazarus. He passed me a can, and I took a deep swallow of rum. "You can see now. No more of the spectacles, go and see." I grabbed the spectacles and tore them from my face, shedding a horrible disfigurement. St. Lazarus laughed like a chorus of hyenas, beating off a murder of pied crows from a fresh kill on the African savannah. "Tomorrow you can leave, but you must return by nightfall. Always before the sun sets must you be in the palm-frond hut." St. Lazarus took a long gulp of rum and poured us two more drinks.

I sat stone faced and stoic, drinking rum under a bent palm tree. He took the pot from me and put it in his lap. He grabbed his bag of bottles, opened it, and put each one upside down in the sand. They were the bottles of small fish and sea creatures from the palm-frond hut. "Tomorrow you can go and see, but you must know where and what you do." I looked at the magisterially unpleasant St. Lazarus quizzically and realized that I had played his game and won some sort of freedom for my eloquence. I could wander only to the places that he was to tell me.

"Where can I go and what can I do?" I asked as St. Lazarus finished organizing the bottles. He looked at me and that smile appeared again, whimsical yet dangerous.

"Let us see what grows out of your lies." He took the earthen pot and grabbed at a handful of bottles. He began to laugh slowly and mutter things to himself as he poured a small amount of each bottle into the soil in the earthen pot. "Red fish water gives truth, yellow fish water gives light, the water of the king crab's leg gives strength." He muttered this nonsense as he watered the soil with the murky salt water. He looked like an ancient shaman as he toiled over the pot, the shadows from the flickering firelight seeming to peck at his face and body like vultures. A chill of dread consumed me. He laughed more and more, talking gibberish and pouring bits of this and that into the pot. Finally, he grabbed the black bottle. "Some of the soul of the fishmonger's wife will give us life," he said as he poured her soul over the soil. "Now you see what blooms, gives us directions on how you will spend your days, and remember always to come to the palm-frond hut before the sun no longer shines."

We both huddled over the earthen pot. He smiled anxiously, as if knowing what would happen. I was expecting nothing. I looked but did not see anything. "Whoo, God Almighty!" he exclaimed. "Can you see that?" I looked as hard as I could and saw nothing.

"No, I don't see anything." I looked him in the eyes and asked, "Do you expect something to grow from the cigar I just planted?"

"Yes," he said and continued to stare deeply into the earthen pot. "You can see now; open your eyes, breathe, and look." I squinted and strained, looked at it upside down, sideways, right-side up, picked up the pot and scrutinized it like a finicky spinster looking over a fish dinner. Then when I was about to tell St. Lazarus he was wrong, I saw it—a tiny bud—and it was growing. It was growing into a beautiful plant with wonderfully twisted leaves, a multitude of green and yellow and blue paisley patterns. It was soft like the most delicate fern, yet it had thorns like a rose, and at its apex there began to sprout what looked to be a flower. I touched the bud and the flower moved with me, gently pushing my fingers back. "Excellent," I whispered to myself.

St. Lazarus looked at me and shuffled closer, whispering in my ear. "To be free to choose your destiny, you must do what the flower tells you." I saw no depth in the aberrant eyes of St. Lazarus, for he had been here since the beginning, his soul all but gone, taken by fornicating with the sea on full moonlit nights, and too much rum. "What you must do is in the flower. Take it, but remember to never, never use your heart." St. Lazarus appeared serious in his words, but I learned never to take the words of a remarkably screwy and unwonted creature at face value. I hopped up toward the pot since I was squatting down, and I made my way to the plant. I carefully felt the plant with my fingers; it was born of my lies, so it was inherently a part of me. I slowly put my hand around the flower and plucked it. Opening my palm, I saw that the flower was merely a carefully thought-out origami rose made from newspaper. The most beautiful example of which I had ever seen. I pulled on what was left of the stem and the flower unraveled itself. I quickly closed my hand, afraid to see my future too quickly. This was the only chance I would have in this queer realm to gain some sort of independence. I wondered what my task would be. I slowly opened my palm and flipped the sheet of paper over. It only contained two words: SEDUCE PERSEPHONE. I wondered what this meant.

As I was about to ask St. Lazarus for insight, he jumped at me and grabbed my head. I was paralyzed. He moved too fast, like a bolt of electricity or the blast radius of a roadside bomb. He wrapped his four-foot-long arms around my curly-haired head and covered my mouth with his sweaty palm. It tasted like some brined and spoiled pickled eggs. I gagged and choked. His nose pressed against mine and he began to speak. "Tomorrow you will go; now you must sleep and dream." He took a deep breath and exhaled into my nostrils. His breath was acrid and bitter, like sniffing pure ammonia mixed with spoiled oil and rancid butter. My throat began to tingle, and slowly, very slowly, I began to sink away from his tight grip, into a deep, deep sleep.

The mother, the father, and the friend

2

Ah, I was dreaming. To be gone from that place and St. Lazarus was delightful. My eyes were still closed, and I wanted to see where I was slowly and enjoy each movement of my soul. I was alive here. I felt a hot breeze come from all around me, and there was something in my mouth. It felt like a drinking straw. I opened my eyes to find myself on the side of a mountainous desert road, sitting on a reclining lounge chair, drinking champagne through a straw, wearing heart-shaped sunglasses, and with an incredible desire for the ice cream truck to stop by. I was in the middle of nowhere. But I knew this place. If anything remained of my soul's memory, then I had heard it gently speak to me: Argentina. A land of passion; a land wet with earthy pools of sweat from dancing women—wearing loose woven dresses—whose necks taste like warm salted butter, when the consent to kiss is given; and as you embrace each other, the singularity that you both become in wholesome partnership will become surrounded by rats, rats that pick at your ankles, rats of the most foul and depraved ambitions for corruption and power that one can imagine.

I sat on the lounge chair finishing my cold champagne. There were no cars driving along this road. I re-adjusted my fake jewel-encrusted, heart-shaped sunglasses and was about to get up. As I rose, a beautiful black and yellow canary jumped out of the laurel bush next to me and landed on the edge of an old empty blue children's swimming pool that I had failed to notice. The small wonder was out of place in the aridity of this desolate landscape, it showed no fear and gracefully came closer hop by small hop. My heart, who shows itself at times like this, wondered out loud where this bird came from. My heart felt pity for this poor creature; I knew it would not survive the harsh climate or perilous wildlife that seek to ingest it. My mind feels different. It quiets all my energies down. Shouldn't I feel honored that such a beautiful bird has graced me with his presence? I spoke to myself. "If I were a bird, would my song be melancholy or pleasant? Surely, though, if I were a bird, my plumage would be boring," I said as I got up and started walking towards the hills.

However, deep down somewhere in my guts, I knew the rats would tear the thing apart—leaving opalescent thin hollow bones, a rotting cloaca, and ripped golden feathers—its disjecta membra[7] would slowly turn into wet rotten earth: A home for maggots and ants.

I knew this was Argentina, and I knew where I would have to walk to see my her/him, this duality I had come to know, which graced me with filial love while I slept. I must walk to the old willow tree with a trunk so thick that ten men holding hands could not reach around its circumference. Where the many waters, the interlacing streams, became a small river, with deep clear pools, that at dusk would reflect the pink flames of the fiery sunset, the tips of the flowering water reeds, and thick white clouds like a flowing mirror, a never-ending reflection of our world, deep through the cavernous rocks and off into the horizon, where the world ends. I did not remember my life here, why here? I knew this was Argentina because of the sky. On any given day the sky is always very blue and bright and the clouds are white and puffy. It was summer, and I was still wearing the same clothes I had in the Fortunate Isles, the islands at the end of the western ocean, far from the known world. I was only wearing cargo shorts. I knew it was summer because usually in late January, the alamos, quebrachos, algarobos, and other trees and shrubs, even twigs, drought stricken and dried for a year, begin to bud in green and yellow bursts that break the monotonous desert landscape, sprouting randomly, life spurting forth from the womb of the Earth.

---

[7] . Referenced from the section of dialog found in *The Blue Carbuncle*. Henry Baker, a museum researcher with a large head, who does not have gas laid in his house, uses this archaic and scholarly language to refer to the remains of a Christmas goose that was found to have a valuable gem in its crop. However, geese do not have "crops" as other birds may have in their natural architecture of composition.

It was a blistering summer's day. The bloated sun that sleeps burning over the land evaporated the horizon in front of me, behind me, and in all directions. If I could remember correctly, I was somewhere near the tree; behind me lay the long straight line of faintly glimmering lights on Route Seven; ahead of me were the Andes mountains.

A memory shot into my mind. It was of an old life, maybe years ago, maybe yesterday. Crossing a barren and wasted vineyard, penniless, with mud underfoot, at nighttime, under a bright moon, only thinking of visions and dreams, hoping for a companion in my utter solitude. I had experienced beautiful tranquility that night. I had seen this place many times and always returned to it. I had drunk in all of Argentina. I had seen the beauty on the face of a poor deformed gypsy beggar child, scratching out a meager living on the streets, bloodying his tiny fingernails, usually for his parents, darting through café tables, dodging the swats from angry waiters. But I never worried for that child; this is the land of the gaucho, where inglorious and false piety meets Catholicism and Godlessness, and one only tenuously believes in the word of one's comrade since a lie has always been easier to hold onto. This is the land of dreams—or once was, if memory serves me right—the land of wine and heroes, a land where men would rather stab you in the belly than accept an apology. That's why I was here.

I walked for what seemed ages, but the sun never moved. I was accustomed to having those awful heavy glasses pressed against my nose, my neck always weighed down. Realizing that there was much more to see than my bare feet shuffling against pebbly asphalt, I twisted my neck up and saw the hand of God. I felt the Earth shift. In their immensity and splendor, the high Andes mountains were pressing against my chest. I took a very deep breath, for I was very high in the hills, as close as I would ever be to God, and I just hoped I could breathe in a small amount of the divine. To share a bit of this small creation we call "Gaia," our Mother Earth. I took in air and felt my heart slowly begin to beat again. "Oh to be alive in a dream!" The thought reached the tip-top of my lungs, and I heard myself shout it. I was close to the willow tree. My heart pounded faster. I began to run. With every step, a minuscule amount of memory began to trickle down into my cerebellum. The wind against my face brought feeling, cold air shook my bones, while the sun baked me from above. This is the only place you can get a sunburn while the cold wind whips your skin. I knew that I was one who remembered. Why could I not know my mother-father's name? I knew that constant itch below my skin was them. I think of them, or they, as *ad infinitum*, for I had come to know them well in my dreams as a vision of wholeness in their androgyny and dichotomy. Forgetting, for me, is an impossibility. I ruminate. I think with my heart too much. Thinking on emotion is the bane of my existence.

I ran a steady cadence, each footdrop matching a ventricle in my heart opening and closing, each breath, in and out, in a slow but strong thudding as my bare feet pounded the asphalt. I was chopping up and cutting my feet on pebbles and rocks, panting, and I was being pulled towards them, if only for the reason of some sanity and expanse, since the limited space with St. Lazarus was confined, oppressive, and humid with the wet scent of rot. I saw the top of the enormous willow tree, and then slowly, as if the ground let out a sigh, there they were.

Everything I saw or had seen, the willows, pines, and alamos, the watercress growing by the side of the crystal-clear stream, the mountains and the rivers, the condor riding the wind, up, up, up, into infinity, became trivial. They were sitting underneath the wide falling branches of the gargantuan willow tree waiting for me, wearing a short-cropped blond haircut, sides shaved, plaid knee-length shorts, a black tee shirt covered in acrylic paint, ankle socks, children-sized Chuck Taylors, and a few tattoos that had a meaning deeper than creation itself, leaning on the tree, smoking a long menthol cigarette, looking out into the mountains. I stood awestruck; happy to witness this wholeness once again, and gratefully proud, for they were my only, and truest friends.

I felt a shock of anxiety, not because of anything beautiful or gracious, and the moment of hesitation grew larger and longer, almost untenable, for no reason but a rash of overthinking on what I was to say when I spoke to them. Frozen and tense, my heart beat harder, this time rapid and short, the veins in my hand bulging, the pit of my stomach quivering, and the stillness of the air bringing a stinging numbness down my spinal cord. I slowly bent down on one knee, picked up a handful of loose dust, and threw it into the air. "A gift for the wind," I muttered, still choking down air from my hard run. The wind began to speak from mountain top to mountain top. Its cracks and moans echoed in some dead language only the gods could understand. It finally hit me, salacious and moving. The winds that fan the passions of everyday ordinary men blew over me hard, pushing me to face my fears. I sprang forward, born to move again, passionately—

I'm using the word "passionately" in the Latin sense: "to suffer."

I walked over slowly, wiping the sweat from my brow, running my fingers through my thinning oily hair, slicking it back, kicking a few stones with my busted-up feet, and stepped onto the cold grass by the tree where they stood beside a once-grand fire pit. I stood next to them, croaked out a tense and meek "hello" almost under my breath as they did not look at me; they only stared vacantly at the ashes in what must have been a great and noble fire, where all gods may have danced to the pipes of Pan, and drank with Dionysus.

"I wonder," they said in a diatonic third interval voice, "I wonder how the ashes of dead embers still retain the shape of the burned wood, now consumed, held up only because the wind has chosen not to blow them into disrepair and scatter them onto the land." They finally looked up into my face. Their amber hair, tinged golden from the Andean sun, twisted from the top of their head and curled a tiny bit. They cut their locks with a short dull knife, or the short scissors of a rusted Swiss army knife; all uneven chops and bits of bare skin showing, they had cut scabs and sheared skin bare. Their face was both male and female, a boyish mix of scarred femininity, and the furrowed brow of a boxer, with wispy and badly shaven chin and cheek stubble in uneven patches. They somehow looked smooth, like deeply toasted porcelain, shining as if they were created out of air and held together with the finest particles of precious metals, and pricelessly worn over ages—a rich patina glazed ancient earthenware pottery. They glowed like the polished crystal pebbles one finds in a river and were as subdued as a rare piece of very worn sea-glass. The sad pools of their eyes, green and blue and brown, told tales of suffering and catharsis, eons of troubles and wisdom not found in books, of their children—caring for all their daughters and sons—and of sharing the collective sins of humanity. They raised their small hand and grabbed the long pungent menthol cigarette from their lips and ripped it in half, lighting the other end with the ember and passing me half of the strong tobacco. "You should smoke," they said as they softly took my hand and pulled me to sit down. "There are always too many things to worry over, so a smoke, at least, is an appropriate method of self-harm; every creature must have some vice. It is the way we make the world turn," they said as I sat down. "All great men and women have a hidden vice, at least with smoking, it is out in the open." They smiled graciously, showing stained teeth, while patting down the grass by the tree trunk to make a habitable depression in which to sit. Each thump of their small palm rung out and jangled their intricately braided leather bracelets—strung with small pewter and copper trinkets, like small bells—jingling like the keys on the pocket watch chain of an old man with too many responsibilities, or the clangs from bells tied to a distant pair of ewes, lost in the mountain meadows, aimlessly running from the wolves and bears.

"Why did you come here today? You look like an absolute disaster, cut-up bloody feet, shirtless, and covered in sweat," they said in a monotone voice that was soft, yet somehow echoed over the mountains and streams and made the wetland grasses sway as if they were being gently wafted through by an alpine zephyr. They put out their menthol cigarette and handed me the butt. It had "Madame Chartreuse Sweet 67" printed around its circumference; the Sweet 66's are St. Lazarus' brand of choice. I threw the butt into the large fire pit and thought of why I came to them again, always in my dreams. I remembered once—maybe it was in a former time, or many years ago, or maybe it was only yesterday—a vision of them: "The [heavens were opened and the whole] creation [which is under heaven] shone and [the world] trembled. [And I was afraid, and I] saw in the light...a likeness with multiple forms...and the likeness had three forms.'[8] One form was lost in my memories, it seems for eternity; but two of the forms were they, or her for '...[she is]...the image of the invisible, virginal, perfect spirit... She became the mother of everything, for she existed before them all, the mother-father [matropater].'[9] They looked at me directly in the eyes. As they wiped their palms on their thighs, they slowly raised their small hand and patted me on the head. "Señor Matanza, my dear, 'there is in everyone [divine power] existing in a latent condition... This is one power divided above and below, generating itself, making itself grow, spouse of itself, daughter of itself, son of itself-mother, father, unity, being a source of the entire circle of existence.'[10] That is why you are here, and that is why you came to see us and to be with us again."

They slowly put their hand on the stem of a pure white thorny mountain flower and gently raised their fingers to pick off a small red and black ladybug that was softly asleep in its petals. They let it crawl to the tip of their finger and blew a small puff of breath to set it flying. The ladybug buzzed for a

---

[8] . Apocryphon of John 1.31-2.9, in NHL 99.
[9] . Apocryphon of John 4.34-5.7, found in NHL 101.
[10] . Hippolytus, ref 6.17.

brief second and came back to their chest, walking over acrylic paint stains and tears on what seemed like a hand-me-down, child-sized black tee shirt. I sat quietly and wondered how a being of such grace lived under an old willow tree. They again picked the ladybug off their chest—both a male and female chest, with one breast hanging loose against their shirt, a nubile and fluid body—and placed it in my open palm. "This ladybug is like you: it comes and goes and lives a life only seeing the next flower petal to land on, as you have always been, as a child, and adult, and the tiger you once were, always looking for something permanent yet never finding within yourself any peace or wellbeing. Those things have followed you here and will do so always."

I held the tiny creature and placed it in the soft grass on the banks of the seven waters that met to form a crystal river. It left my grasp and I watched it fly aimlessly, as jerkily as a nervous bird being taken for a ride by the wind. "I never understood reality, or where I was, or where I belong. I know that," I said to them as we both reclined our heads, our arms folded behind us, onto our palms. "What I know now is that we make of ourselves what we want, and that we become what we think, and that by any God-given grace we may reach a place of influence. Maybe I have wasted my life, maybe I have not, but ideas become reality, and dreams become real." They smiled a coy smile I didn't expect and looked at my face with a serious and clear smile.

"I know this," they said. "I am in you and have been forever, and always will be, "[I] am [Protennoia the] Thought that [dwells] in [the Light]... [she who exists] before the All... I move in every creature.... I am the invisible One within the all."[11]

They knew me, who I was, who I am, my struggle to identify that I have carried time and time again, a restlessness that I suffer from in shared struggle with them since they are in me. To me, as a man, they represent my femininity and my masculinity; they are the wholeness that we all must one day become as complete persons. "What should I call you?" I said as I thought of a way to address my friend.

"I will tell you what I am first, then you can decide what to name me if you wish, my dear child, my dear Señor Matanza." They took a breath and reached into their pocket pulling out a small round flat green stone, passing it over and through their knuckles like a gambler may with a large half-dollar, and threw it over my head onto one of the seven streams, skipping it for what seemed like miles. "I am the first and the last. I am the honored one and the scorned one. I am the whore, and the holy one. I am the wife and the virgin. I am (the mother) and the daughter... I am she whose wedding is great, and I have not taken a husband... I am knowledge and ignorance... I am shameless; I am ashamed. I am strength, and I am fear... I am foolish and I am wise... I am godless and I am one whose God is great."[12]

I sat and thought for a quick moment about how to encapsulate their words into a name for my mother-father. I looked up to see an Andean condor ride an updraft far into the sky until he became only a speck hidden among the bright white puffy clouds. I saw the wholeness of breadth of this

---

[11] . Trimorphic Protennoia 35.1-24, in NHL 461-462.
[12] . Thunder, Perfect mind 13.16-16.25, in NHL 271-274.

creation and the beauty of them as they quietly sat, the breeze ruffling their loose tee-shirt like the sails on a ship. Looking into the giant fire pit, I wondered what coursed through their mind, since they were whole and loved by God.

"Can I call you The Babirusa?" I said nervously. "It means one who is loved by God, or it's a fat wild pig that's own tusks grow into its own brain, killing it. I'm not sure. I have forgotten."

They smiled and patted my head once more, like a true friend would, then they grabbed both of my hands. "So it must be and so it is. I like that name," The Babirusa said as they slowly stood up and pulled another Madame Chartreuse Sweet 67 out of a black and purple tin, lit it, took a seemingly fathomless puff, broke it in half and gave me a taste of the strong medicine they smoked. It was like inhaling fresh forest herbs and had the aftertaste of sweet vermouth with lemon and soda, as earthy as kissing the tears off a lover's lips, and as bracing as holding a bare breasted woman, whose hair smells of camphor and mint, under a star-filled autumn sky.

Every time I dream—if it is a dream, if it is another reality then so be it—the logic of this place escapes me, but The Babirusa has been here since the Earth was young. During the struggle with the Titans, they saw and lived and loved; a triptych: three parts, both of matropater, and one more that I cannot know. As I thought of their history, I wondered at the dances and feasts the gods had. I thought of their undoing and demise, for the exact time and place of Jesus' birth is unknown; but I did know, or have heard from credible sources, that Pan was there, hidden behind stacks of grain and hay across from the Christ child's manger; he knew then and there that he was going to die. I heard that that night, after much sadness, he took the little drummer boy, played his pipes one last time while drinking mulled wine from the sweet grapes of Vinland, and danced as the drummer boy beat a strange and arrhythmic tempo. Cries of sadness were heard from the nymphs of the forest and of the streams, and the long-eared desert foxes all bowed their heads in sadness; and after much drinking and dancing on a night where the moon was full and stars blazed blue fire from the sky, bats weaved into and out of patterns of sacred geometry, and the date palms were ripe with fruit, Pan took one last step from the drummer boy and vanished into oblivion, never to be heard from again.

I looked at The Babirusa nervously, only because they had been here and loved so many and created so much. I took another inhale of the delicious Madame Chartreuse Sweet 67 and gazed at a sea of beautiful wildflowers; tall grasses that gave way into the mountainous valley, an ocean of colors struck on for an infinity; "the madness of Van Gogh." I thought to myself.

The bees buzzed by, and the birds sang songs of love, while the wind made marvelous music rustling the drooped leaves of the willow tree. "The Babirusa, am I a good or bad man? Have I suffered the anxieties of lost love and fallen into hatred and unkindness? I see that here in the ether, things are real, and if they were or were not before, was I at least kind to others?" The Babirusa smiled kindly and softly ran their fingers over the grass by their crossed legs.

"Señor Matanza, my dear friend, you were torn, and you were broken, and you still are. You were a tiger and one who pitied none; a strong man, yet weak and afraid to love.

Judgment and suffering are relative, my dear. What may have been suffering to you may not be to me. As you grew and your heart lost bits and pieces, and chunks were torn from it, it only meant that the vacuum, and the expanse left, the hole so to speak, grew large enough to hold even more love; yet you never took the chance to fill it. You were only held together with grace, as a beautifully shattered piece of pottery is mended with molten gold." The Babirusa seemed sad when they finished telling me my histories, or of what matter I was composed, for we are all some kind of matter, and I knew deep down that as a tiger I must have sipped the waters of every fluvial artery on Earth; the abhorred Styx, the sorrow of the Acheron, the cries and lamentations of the Cocytus, breathed in the flames of the Phlegethon, and finally drunk from the slow and winding Lethe where my cupped hands dripped my last memories of pain, sadness, joy, and love from my pursed lips, the water sweet like honeyed milk and cinnamon and the kisses from women with persimmon-bitter mouths who may have once loved me, only to find themselves alone. I realized then and there that my ethereal matter had consisted of cruelty and loathing. I felt a strange longing, a pull for repentance while I nervously and compulsively played with the button on my cargo shorts.

"The Babirusa," I said. "Thank you for being kind to me. Thank you for being my friend. I will be your friend as best I can." What seemed like an old wound came back into my memory. "I just want you to understand how I am thinking: there are people who prey on the sensibilities of the most vulnerable, stick at them like a fly in their ear, telling them inveracities about a rival's accomplishments either from feelings of jealousy or threat. I applaud their efforts, since regardless of vulnerability or naïveté, if someone chooses to not befriend you without studying you, then they are a waste of time and should be immediately removed from your life like a gangrenous limb." The Babirusa's Davinci-like smile disappeared for a fraction of a second.

They said in a voice that carried like a whisper of a thunderstorm over all the high mountains, "I am sorry that somewhere in times past you have felt those things. I'll repent those sins for you and forgive you, but the one who must forgive truly and honestly is oneself."

They effortlessly got up from sitting cross legged, made small footprints as they walked around the far side of the giant willow tree, returning with a large stainless steel salad bowl and a handkerchief tied up loosely, holding a few bottles and brown paper parcels. They walked towards where the seven streams met and dipped the bowl into the cold water, almost tripping over their tiny stride as they walked back to where I was planted in the earth, rooted in silence, and thirsty for a memory. They placed the oversized bowl at me knees and opened the handkerchief. It held a glass-blown bottle of oil made with different colored glass like a child's favorite marble, and the packets as they untied them were filled with envelopes of spices and incense. They, silently and without asking, grabbed my two cut-up, bloody feet and washed them in the bowl. The ice-cold glacial water woke me, the dull throb of my feet slowly went away. They dried my feet with the handkerchief, picked at the flaps of torn skin, and poured oil over them, rubbing in powerful spices and incense. I said nothing. Slowly, the dull ache began to return, the wounds began to bleed once more. They looked as if astounded for the first time in eons. The Babirusa kept rubbing oils, herbs, mulled wine and rinsed them over and over with an expression of curiosity and grief. They scrubbed with laurel leaves, and strips of bark from the first cedar discovered by Epimetheus in the Wadi Qadisha [13], in the center of the Bsharri.[14] They scrubbed ever harder, vigorously; I bled more and more. The water of the bowl turned pink, then brick red and purple, as drops of blood dripped into it like ink from a fountain pen.

"You cannot be cleansed my friend. These wounds are deep. The dirt is thickly caked on, the muds of many places, the earth of many graveyards, the filth of many crimes; you will never find redemption."

I felt a deep sorrow, a sorrow I lacked the empathy and vocabulary to express. The Babirusa saw my sadness.

"We still have tonight to remain friends and celebrate whatever is left for us."

They looked into my eyes and grabbed my hands with such strength that I had never felt so powerless yet loved at once. "I am the voice... [It is] I [who] speak within every creature... Now I have come a second time in the likeness of a female, and have spoken with them... I have revealed myself in the thought of the likeness of my masculinity."[15] I knew I loved them in that

---

[13] . The forests in Lebanon that are considered holy,
Mentioned in the *Psalms of King David, 104:16,* and have been used to argue that Lebanon has existed as an Ethno-Religious State multiple times throughout history.
[14] . The cedar forest that contains the *Cedars of God.* Worshipped by ancient orders of Christian monks—leaders of other past and modern faiths; monotheistic, polytheistic, and pagan—found within the *Wadi Qadisha.*
[15] . Trimorphic Protennoia 42.4-26, in NHL 465-466.

moment, and I suffered a full and happy heart. "I am androgynous. [I am both mother and] father since I copulate with myself... [and with those who love] me... I am the Womb [that gives shape] to the all... I am Me, the Glory of the mother."[16] They blushed for a brief second, or I thought they did. I stared at them and took them in, holistically, in their glory and scope. "Señor Matanza," they said. "Sit with me and let's talk like kind friends we used to be, learn how to tell our story, which will end tonight. Remember me and speak well of me, remember to be my friend." I did that evening in that dream, I was held in deep filial compassion, kindness, and engaged in heartfelt conversation by my friend—my mother-father—drinking vodka cranberry highballs and listening to their pain: Minutes passing as slowly as the space between the distant galaxies that shone in the light blue deepness of their eyes.

---

[16] . Trimorphic Protennoia 45.2-10, in NHL 467.

Persephone the lonely

3

Roses have been mentioned throughout history as vehicles of passion. Since the day we began to associate the thorns and flowers with the sufferings of love, there have been many roses who have come and gone, shed their petals upon a bed for two young lovers or adorned a tomb, or who have gone unseen in a thicket collecting dew. One such rose was Persephone. Her name wasn't really Persephone; her real name had become lost and entangled with the ghosts in her past, catching dust in a web far away where men ceased to be. She was permitted to live only in rumors and hearsay. A mystery she was, a specter. Only when floating through the ether may one hear a tale of her.

Well, Persephone found herself wilting, her stem had been slowly breaking. Her once-beautiful and shiny leaves were beginning to writhe into dried knots, and her once-sensuous petals were slowly starting to fall, one by one, onto the ground, just like the many tears she had cried, over and over, because she knew no one would save her from the abuse, gabble, and violence of the busy chitter chatter of the fishmonger and his wife.

Persephone opened her eyes slowly. The syncopated drumming and thumps of enormous raindrops on the precarious tin sheet roof above her head had stirred her from her mid-morning nap. The rusty roof apparatus was vibrating, whizzing and ringing like a cheap dollar store battery-powered doodad that poor children get for their birthdays. Her head lay on her left arm as if it were a comfortable feathered pillow. A pillow fat, lumpy, and soft, conforming to her head and hair, molding to her form. She imagined that. Imagination was her only comfort here. Her dark hair spilled onto the straw bedding on which she lay and shone as bright and as strong as the hair on the most beautiful glass dolls from the Orient. The bedding smelled like urine; the straw would heat up and steam on cold nights, occasionally flaming up and burning her hair covered hammer toes. She puckered her strong, chapped, cracked, and scabbed lips, bit into her rubbery bicep and muttered a resigned melancholy oath, never exclaiming it in anger, only in sadness. "So we find ourselves here again, huh?" she whispered to herself still lying across the straw bedding. Her fingers tapped a puzzling staccato rhythm onto the palm wood floor. Her other hand was outside of the bamboo bars of her cage. Peering at her slender fingertips wet with rain, she re-focused her eyes on the movement behind her hand. Right in front of her outstretched fingers, a tiny black bird scurried across the jagged volcanic rock, stepped uncomfortably into the air, rose noisily, flapping its brand-new feathered appendages, and flew for the very first time. Persephone gazed with wonder and longing, tears welling up in her eyes. She quickly regained her composure, for she had become hard inside and not prone to tears. Unlike in her first few days, when the spectacle of her shame in the cage, her food trough and bucket, when the fishing nets cut her; that day when she became completely addled by the scope of her reality. "I wish that was me," she stated as she turned on her back and stared at the rivets in the cage's tin roof leaking drops of water slowly onto her, wetting her, each drop falling like the beat of a timpani in an orchestra; she alternated her finger taps to coincide with the rhythm of the rain. "That bird will fly off, live a long untroubled life, travel the world, maybe nest in the spires of the Hagia Sophia, the highest perches in the Andean mountains, or the thatched roof framing on the lowliest of peasant huts—chirp its dreams and ideas to the strongest of eagles, foxes, condors, and vultures fearlessly and as equals— roost with his lover breast to breast on cold nights, peck small kisses to his featherless hatchlings, and teach them the ways of the wind. I know this."

Persephone interlaced her thick-skinned thin bony fingers, stretched out her arms with a sigh, plucked stray strands of straw that stuck to her clothing, and put her hands behind her head. She was wearing an old pair of hand-me-down cargo shorts that reached down to her knees. The shorts, so worn, had lost their pockets, although their imprint remained stitched at her thighs. She wore a short-sleeve, button-down which she had tied off right at the midriff, exposing every boney and now flattened and squaring curve, and an odd-looking paunchy beer belly. She had an unusually large outie belly button, like a starving pot-bellied New Guinean toddler. The shirt was striped white and green and had a blue and white ribbon sewn onto the pocket. The buttons had disappeared long ago, and the fishmonger's wife had replaced them with small round stones, fastened by threads of woven sea grass. On her feet she wore woven sandals with a palm-frond sole, exposing her thickly knobbed hammers toes, with wisps of black hair on each knuckle.

Her beauty was by no means ordinary, for she was not an ordinary woman. Her body had been shaped from toil, days upon days of laboring for the fishmonger and his wife. She had become strong; the baby fat that surrounded her cheekbones and belly had been burned away. When she felt the pangs of hunger every night, she would always whisper to herself, "Like a piece of fat burning in a fire, the life of a person must hinge on their own consumption." Her strikingly weird body was only matched by the geometric oddness and complexity that was her face. The fishmonger and his wife would spread rumors to the crabs and starfish, and just about anyone or anything that could listen, that Persephone was born with a cloaca, like a bird, and her mother was half otter and half fox, and that her father was friends with the great turtle[17] on who the weight of the Earth lies, and the snake[18] that seeks to devour it.

Persephone, now, had sad dark brown eyes. They did not penetrate and seek anymore, no longer constantly learning and

---

[17] . Section of a Creation Myth: J.L. Borges, *Encyclopedia of Magical Creatures*. The author does not remember where it was, or what entry it was located in.

[18] . Section of a Creation Myth: J.L. Borges, *Encyclopedia of Magical Creatures*. The author believes that the "snake" reference is in a separate entry than the reference of the turtle. He would rather work off memory.

inquiring like they used to. Her eyes just took things in with a relatively lamentable sigh. Her nose was pleasant and had the quaint predilection of turning up when she sneezed and smiled. It met well with her thin greasy scarred pink lips, which had chapped and become hard like scabs under the hot dry sun.

"Wife!" yelled out Persephone. "Wife, your husband has not fed me and you have not bandaged my hands!" She was in agony, although she did not show it. Her stomach lapped at itself like a wolf cub. Her fingers were cut from mending steel fishing nets, which the fishmonger used in the deepest part of the sea to fish for the abominations the gods had discarded. She had the hands of a thin, jaundiced, alcoholic sailor.

"Oh, young mistress, you have awakened! Let me get the lock off your box." The fishmonger's wife fumbled with the lock, chewing on an overripe, rotting papaya. The juice dripped off her chins and onto her chest. Her fingers were soaked in nectar. They glistened in the cloud-drizzled sunshine. Chunks of fruit were on her knuckles. It looked as though she'd just gutted a fish.

Persephone rose when the hag removed the tin roof from the cage. She winced as her fingers grasped the bars on her way up. "Ah, let me see, girl, your hands," the hag said as she smiled, showing no front teeth whatsoever. Her diet consisted of rotten fruit and spoiled fish—whatever could be mashed into pulp by her gums. Persephone groaned in revulsion. The fish hag held both of Persephone's hands palm up by the wrist and took a long look, examining them. "There is nothing here salt water can't cure," she muttered, turned, and began walking away. As she walked from the cage to a rock cave whose entrance was shrouded by palm leaves, and had fishbones littered all around its entryway, and a fire pit with a hanging pot, and bamboo stakes driven into the ground, with fish hanging, covered in flies, waiting to dry, she said, "Make sure you mend all the nets for the fishmonger by sunset, and go sit in the sea for your wounds when you're done."

Having heard her duties for the day, and seeing the sun begin to break the undulating silver and gray curves of the bottom of the clouds, Persephone stepped out of her cage and onto the black volcanic rock sand. Her feet sank in and the sand covered her toes. She was happy to be up again, the sun tanning her skin, now a deep carcinogenic brown. She placed her hands at her hips for a moment, and then began to run circles around her middle. She began to hear soft murmurs, and they began to get louder. The uncomfortable groans from her abdomen roared as she stood ankle deep in coarse sand. Suddenly, she felt a sharp tug in her belly, as if it were a drum skin being tightened. "Wife! You have not given me a scrap! I will surely die today if you do not feed me!" Persephone was boiling over and livid, yet this scenario happened all too often.

"I did leave you food, stupid girl, but you have stepped on it!"

Persephone lifted her foot to find the rotten, half-eaten papaya covered in black sand. It was a revolting sight. She reached down and picked it up. She brushed off some sand, and she blew off the fruit fly maggots, yet she could not clean it all. "Ugh," she muttered under her breath, disgusted. She was too stoic and proud to endure this mocking and hypnotic toxicity. She believed that she was being serenaded and lulled—intoxicated—by the groaning whoops and death lamentations of Achaean and Danaan pagans, spilling tears over her body, as they offer her quarters as a hecatomb, covering her femurs with her sweet fat, burning it for the gods who will consume her stringy fire-roasted flesh, anointed in olive oil, lemons, and rosemary.[19]

Her situation was precarious. "I know my anima will die here," she said as if almost accepting her fate. She had ignored the spectacle of the fishmonger hiding amongst the stones watching her bathe in the rainwater pools, peering, defiling himself with animalistic delight, the nights locked in the cage, the shame. It was all beginning to become too much for this strong woman to handle, and it was leaving a bad taste in her mouth—a taste like rotten papaya.

She walked calmly to the sea after gobbling up the decomposing fruit. Lying down on her belly, Persephone reached her hands in front of her, dipped them into the cool salty moisture of the ocean, right where the waves first break onto the beach. A strong wave rushed over her hands, stinging her, and passed on top of her head. All she could hear was the rush of the wave, forcefully and violently pushing small repeating sonic booms of water in her ear, like flak bursting in the night sky. Her lips were wet with salt water. The taste was familiar. She remembered a kiss long ago on the neck of a lover now forgotten, an embrace of passion, the only time a man had held her in equality, love, and proper respect.

---

[19] . Inspired by the first few stanzas of *The Iliad* as represented by Homer. Achilles and Agamemnon discuss the fate of the stolen daughter of Apollo's priest, as he pleads to the King to ransom her back (she, having become the most loved concubine of King Agamemnon).

Persephone let her senses become drowned in the sea. For a fraction of a moment, she felt as if she were inside of a beautiful enormous oyster shell, surrounded by iridescent mother of pearl, the waves flowing through her, her heart beating in unison with this grand materfamilias, Ocean. She pictured herself slipping deep down the shell's smooth chamber, sleeping in the seabed. She wanted to be a pearl.

Rubbing her hands together with salt water and sand, Persephone cleaned the dead and scarred tissue on her fingers and palms. She sat up in the cool blue water and ran her hands through her dark hair and placed the bunch of water-heavy silken strands behind the nape of her sun golden neck. The mid-morning rainstorm had given way to an obscenely bright noonday sun. As she sat looking out onto the far-flung and astronomical expanses of the ocean, she began to hear a faint whisper. A sound that she had not heard for years. She could see ripples begin to form on the water's skin. The whisper grew more and more, and soon it was upon her. "The wind!" she exclaimed happily. Persephone almost hadn't noticed since she was still thinking about becoming a pearl. Her body prickled with goosebumps as the cold wind blew over her skin.

"Fish hag!" exclaimed Persephone as she turned excitedly, rubbing her upper arms, embracing herself against the cold wind. The hag did not hear her. She was preparing a supper of aged octopus' eggs and squid beaks. Yet like many things here, these eggs and beaks were most unusual. The octopus eggs measured as wide as the palm of a nine-foot-tall man, almost rotten, smelling of a gangrenous sailor. The beaks themselves had been drying in the sun and were riddled with worms. These were leftovers from the bowels of the trench, so deep in the ocean that the pressure could crush bones. "Wife!" exclaimed Persephone as she ran towards her cage, for she would not go past it; she feared treading near the entrance of the fishmonger's cave. His unusual body scared her, filled her with guilt—feelings of shame that she struggled with—and brought forth in her a vile revulsion that sent the bitter bile from her guts into her mouth and stung her throat.

The fish hag turned and nodded. "What is it, girl?" She was bent over a pot of boiling water and the entrails of dangerous sea creatures. Her enormous frame cast a long dark shadow on the jet-black sand. Her large, long, sagging breasts reached her belly button. One was poking out from the bottom of her burlap blouse. Her shriveled brown sand dollar nipple repulsed Persephone. She shuddered at the thought of aging and watching her beautiful body decay into a monstrosity. "But I have been here for what seems like centuries and not aged," she thought, trying to dismiss the idea of becoming a hag herself. Again, the wind blew strongly over her, a cold wind, wind that did not belong in this plane. Again, she braced herself and rubbed her arms. "Why did I feel a cold wind, hag? There is no wind here, let alone a cold wind." The hag stood up from the pot and looked at her, with a very wide toothless grin. She stuck her tongue out from her missing front teeth and spat out a juicy pit from a wormy peach she was eating. Spittle dripped like strands of honey onto her belly. Her rough skin and ugly features made her face resemble a bloated wet peanut shell.

"Ah, girl, you feel wind, do you? I did not feel wind," said the fishmonger's wife loosely, lisping, lip-smacking the words from the tattered folds in her face. Persephone leaned on her opened cage, her hand grasping the top bar, the broken fishing nets right beside her.

"Are you saying I am lying? I have been here for my eternity and have never felt wind. But today I felt it blow cold chills over me." Persephone began to entertain the notion that she may not have felt it after all. That her body and mind were starving, and she had only thought it happened. "Could the imprisonment and shame be causing me to feel what does not exist?"

"Do not look so confused, young daughter of Jah! You have felt wind over your body today," said the fish hag as she gently lifted a beetle off a rotten piece of baitfish she was planning to introduce into the stew. She put the enormous scarab into her mouth and cracked it open with her only functional molar. "It is because this place is changing," she said, smiling, breathing out pungently in Persephone's direction. "I cannot say much more, because I do not know."

Persephone could not believe what she was hearing. "How is this place changing? How can the excommunicates who populate the Fortunate Isles, fossilized as specters, molt their skin? Are we all serpents?" she thought. "Hag, what do you know of this change?" The hag stirred her pot and did not look at Persephone. The fish concoction bubbled and spat brown liquid onto her lapel.

"The change itself—like you—is only another ghost from history, living in the shadows of the dreams they once had. They wish to sleep, to sleep and learn." Persephone drew shapes into the dark sand with her toe, a graceful writing only she could understand. She was drawing her hopes onto the sand as she imagined what he looked like. "Girl, you look so stupid," muttered the fish hag as she sucked the stains off her blouse.

Persephone looked up deep in thought, pondering who had moved and mastered the wind. "Have you seen it, they, or them, hag?" asked Persephone softly.

"No," muttered the fish hag through her fat jowls, stroking the pockmarks on the lumpy cellulite of her mastiff cheek.

There was a long silence while the hag stirred her pot. She was pumping a bellows with her foot. The bellows made the fire jump and grow as if she were injecting each one of the coals with kerosene. The skin on her legs jiggled like the gelatinous leftovers of a cold turkey dinner. Sweaty, hairy, and broad, her shins resembled braised ham hocks. "Ooh this is the stew that you will remember!" stated the fishmonger's wife excitedly. Alas, Persephone was in no mood for the hag's semi-amicable pleasantries and broken attempts at dialog. She hated the fishmonger and his wife. There was no kindness. She was their slave.

Now Persephone let go of the top bar of her cage and sat on her bottom in the sand. She crossed her legs, grabbed the heavy rusted steel fishing nets, and began to tighten each knot. The knots tore into her flesh as she used her mouth and both hands to unwind and recoil the strands. All she could taste was rust. In fact, everything in the world tasted like rust. Her palms and fingers had become accustomed to this work. Only on days when the knots had been loosened by enormous creatures would she have to work in quantity to cause injury to her delicate hands.

Persephone diligently separated the steel filaments and re-braided them with her teeth and hands. "I could use a friend here; in all seriousness, I need to have a decent conversation. I would like purpose and some reason for tranquility in this horrible place." Persephone sighed because she knew that could never be. The fishmonger and his wife would never allow that. "How could I think to be a good woman when stealing is my only way of being fed, when the shame of displaying my body is the only way of keeping the fishmonger from touching me, appeasing his perverted hunger." She put her head in her hands and exhaled deeply, the pressure of her palms over her eyes causing her to see bright lights and shooting stars under her closed eyelids. "I hope for a friend. I wish for a friend. Gods please, please, bring me a friend."

On becoming evil

4

"Awaken yourself, pig, Señor Matanza, you filthy animal!" I tried to fall asleep again, to be with them one last minute, but it was too late. St. Lazarus stood over me. The smell of his rancid breath was like spoiled vegetable oil with the woody aroma of a sweaty man's crotch. "Are you going to make me pick you up and throw you into the fire pit?" he exclaimed jokingly, although I did see his remark as a distinct possibility. I got up onto my feet and looked him dead in the eye. He wasn't seven feet tall after all; he was about as tall as me today. My body looked more dangerous to me, my hands seemed bigger and three times as powerful. I felt myself with my coarse and calloused hands and realized that I was tight and muscular. St. Lazarus crept in close to my face, looked me over, and said, "Confidence can kill you here, Señor Matanza, so you best put your thoughts away in some corner. You may end up hurt." I laughed to myself and reached for the toothbrush that made it onto these Fortunate Isles with me. I handed it to him.

"It says Colgate on it. You need it more than me." St. Lazarus began laughing like the wheeze of a leaking bellows. I stared him dead in the eye. "Colgate" pronounced Col-Ga-Te translated into Spanish literally means "go and hang yourself." St. Lazarus stopped laughing. I walked out of the palm-frond hut and onto the sandy beach.

"Tonight will be a full moon, son. You will drink rum and be wicked with the ocean." I thought for a moment about fornicating with the ocean. I would not disregard my caring and affection and friendship for The Babirusa and go and learn and know the sea carnally, because I could never make love to anyone. I lack the desire. "You will go tonight after the fire skull dance, after we have become stupid with rum, go and have your way with her, for she is a whore and a great deceiver. Spit on her. Become calloused and evil like me." I shuddered in disgust, and I walked towards the sea. St. Lazarus belted out a song, a song with words no person should hear. He rang each word loudly and clearly. The fiddler crab by my feet surrendered itself back into the ocean in disgust. St. Lazarus laughed from his brown pot belly, spittle dripping off his chin. He cried out to me. "Did not you say that you must abuse people's sensibilities, to use and destroy people?" He was right, I did say those things, but I was only worked into that fervor because it was the beginning of my freedom from this place. I hated myself for lying. I hated myself for being with St. Lazarus.

I looked out into the clear day. It was hot, but a breeze made its way over me and cooled my emotions. I could see the sand, a mix of many colors, like a pastel fresco. The sea was a bright green, as clear as the sky above it. They met gloriously out at the horizon where they were eternally bound to each other. The sky was the ocean's only love. Here, St. Lazarus had his way with her and treated her as if she were a harlot, a dirty woman, false and eager to be had. All the sky could do was bring in fierce winds, but St. Lazarus always managed to survive them. I stepped closer and closer to the sea. I began to hear her heartbeat, like mine; waves crashing against the sand were her pulse. She had a beautiful rhythm. I could dance to her. She could move any man to her side, to be in the ocean, but not from lust: from love. I walked into her and sat down. The water was up to my waist. My heart had been beating since I had spent time with The Babirusa, and I was feeling compassion for this poor forgotten goddess who had been enslaved by wicked men's desires to abuse her and take of her. I stuck my head into the tepid water, minnows swam by, my ears filled with water, clownfish darted in and out of rocky crevasses, and a sand dollar had been placed perfectly by my foot. I looked far into her depths and whispered, "Tonight I will come to see you, your love the sky has brought me my heart." I heard nothing but waves, the slow and patient tidal furies that form our coastal landscapes.

I arose from the ocean's wet grasp, shook the brown curly stalks of my hair, and began walking towards the palm-frond hut. I loved the taste of salt from the sea. The brine cleared my senses, and the water had washed me. I took my time with my steps. I wanted time to see the small seashells on the shore, all arranged in a line where the tide had broken. Beautiful colors of browns and pinks and yellows, they dotted the beach as if they were the strokes of a pointillist masterpiece. There were three pieces of long seagrass intermingled in the shells. I took them and sat upon the beach with my back towards the sun. I was glad to be able to see. The sun was very bright. As I sat, I began to weave the three strands of seagrass into one long and perfect braid. I knotted both ends and looped it around my wrist, making a bracelet, to be adorned when I visit the ocean tonight. I lay upon the sand and looked up into the sky. My heartbeat, I could feel it push, contract, and pull the blood through my veins. As bare as the sky was, there was a single cloud, large and puffy; it sat contented near the sun, looking down upon me.

Raising my arms to my sides, I fell backwards into the sand. Like a great and gritty foam mattress it caught me. My toes dug deep into it. "With a few more million years of erosion this sand will feel like flour," I thought. The wind whipped a gentle breeze over me. My wet hair was becoming caked with sand. "Wind!" I exclaimed in a deeper voice than normal. Nothing. Only a steady breeze raked over me. I arched my neck up and looked down at my chest and stomach. I was a few shades lighter than St. Lazarus. Figuring the wind would not respond to my yelling, I grabbed a handful of sand, held it close to my heart, and silently asked a question. "Why have you been helping me?" I threw the handful of painted sand into the air above my head. Just as it was about to fall back down upon my face, the breeze blew it into the heavens. "The wind must have gotten my message," I thought.

I began wondering how the wind could respond to me when he had no voice. The only thing he could enunciate were the whips of a hurricane or the bellows of a windy storm. Sitting, contemplating, wondering how he would present his answer was another mystery this place presented. Closing my eyes, I began to visualize two people dancing. It was a man and a woman. They were very close together, holding each other and moving, sometimes rapidly, sometimes slowly, as if they were making love. Her beautiful legs would wrap around his, and he would slowly bend her over, then they would gracefully jerk each other into more movement. Was this a memory? I had seen this. Tangerine? No, that's not it. Tangelo? No, not it either. Suddenly a breeze came straight into the side of my head. "Tango," it said softer than the softest whisper a kitten can make. "Wind!" I thought. Another stronger breeze went by my face. "I help you because you need a friend, and she told me to," the wind said in a voice that was sweet and melodic, like a woman's voice.

Keeping my eyes closed, I thought of friendship and who "she" could be. There was no breeze for a few minutes. I thought the wind had left again. As soon as I thought that it blew over me forcefully, blowing the caked sand out of my hair.

"Jolene Armitage."

"Wind," I opened my eyes and yelled out. "Who is she?" I heard nothing. I had broken my lines of communication by speaking.

Getting up from the sand with the ocean in front of me, the waves were playing hopscotch in between seashells and rocks, bouncing off the sand, and then back into the ocean whence they came. I turned my back on the sea and walked back into oblivion. Back towards the palm-frond hut. I heard loud banging, metal against metal. I saw flames reach into the sky, almost setting the clouds ablaze. As I walked over to the bent-over palm trees, I could see St. Lazarus squatting by the fire pit. His cheeks were four times their normal size as he blew into the coals, making the flames reach extraordinary heights. He looked like a seasoned trumpeter, his lips pursed, blowing air out at such velocity that he sounded like a boiling teapot. He held a large hammer. It was at least ten feet in length. Its shaft was made of metal, and at its apex it had what seemed to be a very heavy head. It seemed quite unmanageable since he was holding it at its end. Yet he seemed to have complete control of the task at hand since he was gently tapping the head against metal that was resting on a flat stone. St. Lazarus seemed to be meticulously shaping the lines and curves and bending the form into anything he envisioned. He was taming the indomitable nature of iron blow by blow from his blacksmith's hammer. I remembered this tradition. It was a passion. Passion forged from the smoldering coals, passed on from father to son. "Where did you learn to bend metal?" I asked.

"It is part of why I am here," he said as he blew air at the speed of sound. I did not know one could speak while blowing, but apparently St. Lazarus had that talent.

"If I may ask, what are you making?"

He kept banging on the metal, forming the strips into long rectangles. He took a swig of some schwag rum, put a burning ember to his lips, and blew as hard as he could. The rum was instantly vaporized and burst into a jet stream of fire, melting two black pieces of iron together. He cleared his throat and spat onto the sand. "I am making you a chair," he said as he continued banging away at the metal very softly, working out small details.

"Why would I want a chair? I can sit on the rotten log, or the sand. I don't need a chair," I said, gesticulating with my hands as if his chair were useless, swatting away at the idea. He looked at me and smiled, the whites of his eyes like old, stained, yellowish ivory.

"You may not need a chair, but the Señor you are becoming will," he said as he began to laugh from his gut. "Oh, you will," he repeated as he chuckled repeatedly. I was not worried about his cryptic remarks, for the one with no name was looking after me, as was the wind, and tonight after the fire skull dance, and much, much rum drinking, I would finally be able to see the ocean in all her glory for myself.

Tonight is the kind of night that death would roar at you when you weren't paying attention, like some jungle cat about to tear your head off. I'd heard he always approaches from the left when he claims you[20]. I sat on the rotting log, keeping a close ear on my left side. St. Lazarus was in the palm-frond hut clinking and clanking away. I had no idea what kind of mischievous and nefarious things he was attending to. The end of the rotting palm log gave way under my weight, and I fell onto my back. I stared up into the dead and dark night sky. This was not a night for children, or women... well, maybe the stoutest women, amazons and warriors, single mothers, and women whose strength lies in healing when everything around them is busted up. Even the stars themselves had

---

[20] . The author is working from memory. He believes this passage is referenced in the "Yaqui way of knowledge." Carlos Castaneda's ethnographic work on Native American shamanism, the exploration of self and substance through ritualistic and tribal consumption of naturally occurring substances that alter human perception. If he recalls correctly, it is mentioned that "Death comes from the left."

moved onto other places to escape seeing the evil St. Lazarus and I were to perform. Only the moon, bright and full, milky, creamy, and sharp at the edges was shining. It was shining hard. I say hard instead of bright, because the moon did not want to be there watching us either. It had turned its back on us and showed its other side so as not to see our wickedness. The crickets were silent. Only the breaking waves of the ocean could be heard. I wondered about the waves. They first broke upon the sand, pushing you away. Then they pulled back into the sea, sometimes ripping your feet off the sand and rocks, and dragged you in with them. I got up off my back and picked up the pieces of the rotting palm log and threw them into the fire. All I managed was much smoke and little flames. "Do not worry, Señor Matanza." I heard the words muffled, coming from the inside of the palm-frond hut. "I have much wood that can burn bright and hot, and its smoke will convert your soul to ashes." I looked around me and still saw only two bent palm trees. There were no forests on this island, no places for animals to hide, except crickets and blind cave shrimp in the fishmonger's rock holes.

"Where did you acquire such special wood?" I asked vacantly while admiring my new braided grass bracelet.

"Ah, Matanza, it was once the tree of all things, and I was there to take pieces from it."

"Who cut it down?" I asked, wondering who could possibly cut down the tree of all things.

"Ah," he said, "evil, evil, men who I inspired, like I will inspire you tonight. They are easy men; they follow the words of false prophets, credit accounts, men who can't think, stockbrokers." St. Lazarus paused for a second and looked at me, he rubbed his gums with some ground coca leaves and alkaline charcoal powder he kept inside his robes. "Matanza, every man, every little man, every small malignant rat of a man is an underfed and starving Machiavelli. They all wish to be princes yet can't seem to discern the madness from the science, and the religion from the mythos, and the mythos from the ethos, and the pure chrysalis that molds them into flying things." St. Lazarus threw me a chunk of the tree, and I gazed deeply into the lines and features of this dead organism.

I thought how magical tress are. I thought of Dionysus fornicating deep in the forests with sylvan nymphs and spirits and flowering pear trees and cherries. I thought about who Jolene might be, and why she cared. I grabbed a handful of sand and threw it into the air, taking with it the words "Wind, don't fuck with me!" A violent gust blew me ass overhead, and I landed upside down on my shoulders, the pain in the nape of my neck tremendous and sharp. I slowly turned my body over and yelled out, "Dammit! That hurt!"

St. Lazarus was oblivious, for he was preparing the feast and ceremony. "Did you trip over the log, Matanza? You must be more careful, for I need you in tiptop shape."

I rubbed my neck. "Yes, I tripped. I was careless." I would never tell him I dialog with gods. He was pouring and mixing liquids in the hut; it sounded as if someone were urinating into a tin can. The stout smell of the bug juice was enough to inebriate a whale. "I am preparing you a concoction of the ping-pong tit-tal-iest in the nuclear sub."

I was perplexed by his statement. "What?" I asked.

"Don't worry, Matanza, the drunkest man I have ever seen was Japanese. He lost his life and family when the cloud came up and burned them. You will be drunker than he was. In fact, Matanza, you will be as drunk as the deadliest weapon humanity has created is powerful. And when the smoke from the tree of all things turns your soul to ashes, you will be happy here and we will not need the chair." I took in his rhetoric slowly to remember it. I did not want my soul to become ash. I wanted my heart to beat and to see The Babirusa again in a dream, by the river of seven waters in Argentina.

"When will I sleep again?" I asked loudly since St. Lazarus still toiled in the hut.

"You may not sleep at all tonight because the whore of the ocean will keep you busy." I was sad that he thought of her as a whore. She was a goddess of immense complexity that had never been explored to her entire enormity, and it seemed that no man could speak of her womanly idiosyncrasies, because every wicked man that abused her had never taken the time to even ask her name. I knew it. I knew it in my dead but beating heart. Her name may be our "Mother Earth," our home, "Pacha Mama—the breadbasket." Or it could just be "Jolene."

St. Lazarus emerged from the palm-frond hut wearing a black and white ceremonial robe, the bottom half of his face painted like a skull, the top half like a rising sun. The robe was striped black and white with sea grass sewn into its sides, interlacing it like the braids on my bracelet. He had in his left hand a murky bottle of vaporous and stinking booze, and under his armpit he carried three sticks from the tree of all things. In his right hand he carried an old classical guitar that had writing on it in black grease pencil: "De mortuis nil nisi bonum[21]" "'Tis the guitar of the dead, Matanza," he clarified, "from tower to tower, from god to god, they will all hear you tonight. But watch for the backfire on your soul." I looked at him, and he moved me to smile, a slightly wicked smile.

The wind whipped a memory across and into my skull. "I have played guitar before," I said confidently, because deep inside I knew I was good. Once I held it, I would remember.

"But this is the guitar of the dead, son. You will be bound here for all eternity if you do not move me to dance. But first we must move ourselves into fever by drinking and breathing in the smoke of the tree."

The smell of his breath and the open bottle was horrible. "Why does that rum smell so potent?" I exclaimed while tearing up and holding back gags.

"Because it is fermented from a piece of Aphrodite's rotting heart. Because love does not exist anymore, Matanza, she died long ago."

I looked quizzically at him, wondering how love could die. I thought of it as a pillar of all connection. It made me sad to think that love had passed on. "Let's just do what we have to do tonight, Lazarus. Let us play your game, get hammered and

---

[21] . This is a literal translation of an ancient phrase: "*Of the dead speak nothing but good.*" When the author was a young 15-year-old autodidactic student of the classics; he believed that all men and women should at least be honored after passing into oblivion, that what remains are only memories that slowly fade like Gardner's glass negatives; crystallized moments the become sunburned greenhouse windows. After being matured by age, sorrow, and multiple cruelties, he realized that cutting off the tendrils of those who were sadistic, that attach themselves to the contemporary zeitgeist, and disregarding their past humanity is acceptable. However, the lessons that we learn from those who have wronged the humankind should never be forgotten. The only good to be spoken of terrible people, is what lessons and language can stop a reanimation of their prejudiced and abhorrent ideals.

get weird," I said while laughing. He did not know I was not going to fornicate with the sea. He did not know the wind was by my side.

He looked up at me and smiled, his ridiculously ghoulish face contorted by the shadows. "We must converse again, young Matanza; tonight, we shall converse."

"Ah! Matanza the Tigermother! Come here, lad, and drink heavily with me, for I was at table with Dionysus, watched Athena weave. I was the fly in Icarus' ear that told him to fly too close to the sun. I burnt offerings at Delphi, and I have outlived them all, every single one. Waiting by the Christ child's manger, shooing away errant asses, and putting straw down on the little bastard's bed, I was there at the end, when he recklessly urged rioters in the temple, and I bade Pilate to pardon Barabbas. Come drink with me and I will tell you how to ignore them all and live forever."

"I may go have a talk with the ocean instead," I said to St. Lazarus as he was engaging in an improvised and strange physical exercise.

"You have to keep your body keen, Señor Matanza. Once you stop exercising your joints, you pretty much dissolve into putty and bone, so training your body is a condition of life," he said, having finished his last repetition of some weird and gruesome torturous-looking press-up.

"How does one talk to the ocean? I know you have said that you fornicate with her; how does one find her? Is she a woman of attractions?" I said, wondering out loud while I fidgeted with my sea-grass bracelet, sitting on the rotting palm log.

St. Lazarus looked up at me with a jaundiced face and licked his chapped lips while stretching his arms after the press-ups.

"Ah! The ocean is the mother of us all out here in the three islands. She has birthed the monsters of the sea and the beasts of the air. I wouldn't say she is a handsome woman. I wouldn't say she is a woman at all. She is more like a small collection of things, just trivial things that most wouldn't pay any attention to."

I of course never understand what St. Lazarus says, and I must try to take things as they come here; some truths, some mysteries, and some things may not be for me to understand. "A collection of things, eh?" I asked as I smelled my wrist, which smelled fishy and tangy—the sweat leaving greasy dead skin on my wrist from the bracelet.

I walked into the palm-frond hut and looked among the various shelves, found a worn oilskin pouch with a metal tin, opened it, and found it contained cigarettes and a box of Swedish three-star matches. I had heard that those matches are used in all sorts of voodoo and godless rituals by the observers of strange religions and magic. "St. Lazarus!" I yelled loudly. "Can I have these smokes? I enjoy smoking, it seems to calm my appetites."

St. Lazarus nodded in a manner that was unusual for him. "Let it be so, my friend. Those are particularly delicious, made with the finest tobacco from the Indus region conquered by Alexander the Great, and have a feathery white ash and pleasant oriental taste. It tastes like you are kissing a beautiful woman, who you care a great deal for."

I looked at the printed band around the filter-less cigarette. They all said, "Madame Chartreuse Bidi and Cheroot Blend." The tin displayed the words: "The most pleasurable smoke for rat-bastards and sons of bitches."

"Lazarus," I said, having just lit one of the cigarettes, inhaling deeply and blowing out blue rings of thick smoke into the dark night sky. "Was I a good man? I know and am starting to understand that I have reached the end of my passions, and I feel as though I have a flat affect here, that I don't care much about anything. I feel as though, since I know nothing of my past, the absurdity of my present, which at points is troubled by you, or my feelings, do not really matter, and never have and never will."

St. Lazarus was at the fire, poking the embers incessantly, whistling loudly, and occasionally singing old sea chanteys and hymns no proper person should listen to, due to the vulgarity of their nature. Still focusing on the fire, almost transfixed by it, throwing in branches from the tree of all things, he went into a state of quiet, and finally, after a few moments, began to speak. "Señor Matanza, your case is special. I can say that if you wish to learn of your past, you must be wicked with the ocean, maybe tonight, and go and seduce Persephone. For they know of your history. Of gods, of women, of nature and Dionysian hedonism I can teach you much, yet you are not deserving, since you have committed crimes against gods, for which you will never atone, regardless of sipping the waters of the Lethe and forgetting your past. I can say that you were a mother among tigers, one who had a few strips of kindness but chose in the end to let love pass through your fingers, like water when you wash your hands, or the sand of the beach when you run your fingers and toes through it." I inhaled a long drag from the cigarette. It crackled as the strong pungent tobacco smoke felt smooth and cool as it entered my lungs.

"Am I to accept the absurd?" said I as I flicked the ash from the end of my smoke. "Everyone living and everyone not living, should realize how incredibly absurd the real is. For everything happens in the true form. Ideas such as those have been debunked by thinkers past and present; but for us, the real exists, and it is as unimportant as it is for those who still tread mindlessly upon the lands of great powers, empires, and kings. They are still being ruled, either by corruption or an equanimity, but power rests where it always has: In the hands of the few. The few, who you wished to burn to ashes during your time treading those places; but your crimes outweighed your honest and good intentions and thoughts. You saw the truth in the myth of Sisyphus and when you realized those things. You stopped rolling your own boulder up the hill and became a tiger."

I had finished my cigarette and lightheadedly threw the end of it into the fire and watched it catch alight, sending ribbons of blue and purple smoke into the air. I picked out a burning branch from the tree of all things and inhaled the smoke from the ember deeply, hoping to turn my soul to ashes, but felt nothing, and after a few breaths threw the log back into the fire and walked towards the ocean.

St. Lazarus lay with his lower back against the palm log and silently brought out a few mason jars filled with what looked like vegetable matter steeping in water. He opened the lid and took a sip from one of the jars, threw it over to me, and, catching it, I took a large swallow of the pungent herbal brew, refreshing on this hot and dry night as stars shot across the night sky and galaxies were immured into the heavens illuminating the farthest reaches of the ocean. My heart felt heavy, and emotions were swelling up in me. The palm leaves swayed in the wind and the breeze felt cool and pure like nights I may have had far from these shores. I took a swig from the other mason jar, one with a brown, flakey. and gnarled root steeping in the water. It tasted like breadfruit and jackfruit. I thought, "Now I can talk to the gods of love." No philosopher has ever defined it. They have made it a foundation of everything from revolution to grace, to religion, but in that middle space, in the no man's land between theology and science, can be found the philosopher, and for the most part, try as they might, they have not defined pure and unadulterated love—love that, I am sorry to say, I couldn't feel. I stared up at the galaxies and the fires in the sky. I smoked another cigarette. I looked at the waves crashing against the beach sonorously in a complex melody, rhythmically like a heartbeat, an infant's heartbeat in a sonogram. The sounds of the place were almost overwhelming when I shut my eyes to take it all in.

St. Lazarus began to play a song of a long-ago hero that he called the Oblivion Suite.[22] He started on movement VI of his operatic masterpiece, his voice fouling the air with its atonality. However composed, it was a wonderful song of adventure, alcohol, love, and mistrust, a long and rambling epic poem set to chords that were sometimes like scratching the strings with his long yellow fingernails, and at other times harmonic and beautiful such as the most accomplished and

---

[22] . An epic poem written by the little-known songwriter and wordsmith John R. Deigenova, formerly a member of "The Back Porch Consortium of Writers, Thinkers, and Other Assorted Ne-er do Wells." As of now living in Southern Florida, and occasionally making small concert appearances.

well-known airs that I had heard. St. Lazarus stopped playing and looked at me. "You prayed to me once long ago, you prayed to St. Lazarus, and you have stolen the sacrifices for my altar, deep in years past, or lifetimes, when you were rooted strong like a tree in death and murder. That is why you are with me now."

I looked at him and still wondered why everything about life and death meant nothing, yet I took it with a grain of the absurd. The palm trees swayed as if they were listening to Miles Davis' "Kind of Blue" while drinking ginger and bourbon highballs, a little tipsy on the top, but shuddering through their trunks at the bottom, moving as if dancing with each other. The fire crackled, the grog tasted sweet, my smokes were almost herbal and fresh and cold as if I was chewing spruce boughs and mint leaves. The clouds seemed big, puffy, and white, like the most generous serving of cotton candy at a town fair. I traced my fingers through the sand and picked up a handful, rubbed it into my hands, and took another swallow of the sweet groggy water, licking my chapped lips and sighing a deep-throated thank you to the gods for a quiet evening.

"You need to become our storyteller, Señor Matanza," said St. Lazarus as he swallowed a deep swig of grog. "I am making you a chair, so that as you live here with us, you can sit and tell us all of the histories and places we have never seen. You must learn that." I looked at him quizzically and started to doubt my ability as a scribe. "You can be a good person and believe in nothing at all but yourself," he continued. "Remember that. Does common sense trump morality? For no being is born rotten, they must be pickled in filth as babies to become evil, and there is nothing as evil as indoctrination. Know that Tigermother, for as you better learn to tell stories, the more power over all of us here you will have. Make your message true, neutral, and a touch obscure, so it lets us all think as to what your message may be."

I stood far from St. Lazarus and thought about the mythologies and all the stories that I may have heard when I was the Tigermother, what it may have been like. "How can there be a hero in a story if there is no story, if the story is to learn how to tell stories, for instance? When there is no conflict, how can you move someone? There should be no real hero in stories. Most of the time when you meet your hero in real life, they are frail and complicated people who will most likely disappoint you. The only thing worth putting on a pedestal is one's own unique worldview. Nobody can see things like you, you cannot see what others see, everyone's different sufferings and lessons cloud the truth with the subjective. Maybe I will tell you a story about how I see things and remove myself completely from it, only for you to hear my thoughts. I grow tired of heroes, heroines, conflict, and I assume we all have seen too much conflict in our lives. Maybe when I was the Tigermother I saw conflict; but to elucidate one's thoughts instead of a narrative seems esoteric and more apt for the ponderers who still believe in magic, old lore, and are fascinated with the deviance that pours through most people's daily thoughts and goes unsaid between friends for fear of sounding perverse."

I stared off into the distance and seemingly spoke to nobody in particular. "People always talk about time and space, and if it is infinite or not infinite; however, space cannot be annihilated. A line, for instance, can be divided infinitely and one must think about where it starts or where it ends, for there is no beginning to a line, nor an end, and in regards to time, we must think of only the present, which can also be divided infinitely, for there really is no future except our hopes and dreams, and the past is only memory, so you find yourself surrounded by immense space, and living and breathing in the infinite expanse of the present," I said aloud, lost in thought and personal revelry.

St. Lazarus smiled at me and chuckled a hearty, fat-bellied laugh. "One must act as if it were the moral duty of one to do so. That is the idea of deontological ethics. One must embrace their convictions. Socrates couldn't run away with Crito to escape his fate; it was impossible for him, for he loved his state and its laws and justice and acted in the way it was his moral duty to do so. Yours, Matanza, is the duty to run from whatever shred of morality that you may have, to live as the caricature of perversity you design for yourself, to embrace the obligation to be a liar and a rat. That is what you must learn here. You must become the sage of stories and verse, seduce with ideas, twist the truth, become the false and the corrupt."

"I feel nothing of duty here, my man. Only emptiness that nothing can fill," said I, still gazing far off into the nothing. "We all do or did things, sometimes good or bad, but a duty to re-design myself through myth and hedonism, and accepting no judgment for that would be unfair. I can say that never have I judged another. If I were steeped in murder and death, then I could say I was as detached from it as you are from what is holy, good, and virtuous." I lit another cigarette with the three-star Swedish match and let the match burn down till it charred my fingertips. It hurt. "At least I can still feel something," said I, dipping my finger into a small salt-water puddle; getting up and walking towards the ocean, kicking at the incoming waves that were being hurled violently towards the shore. I went in as far as it took to tread water and have only my head floating above it. I lay on my back, floating with my head and toes and belly just breaking the surface, and fell asleep while I was being dragged far out to sea by the currents and the winds.

Aphrodite's rotten heart

5

"Ha, the stars! Those pitiful leftovers from the ancients!" St. Lazarus said as he cast a weary gaze to the night sky, the greasy paint of his face shone, unctuous; enormous drops of sweat were exuding through the thick layers of paint, dripping heavily onto the ground, leaving abysmal sandy craters with a rumbling thud. "Do you see, Matanza? The stars themselves have gone deep into the vacuous amplitude of the Tartarean sky and left our sight! They cannot bear to see their mother ocean weep." I turned my face down and looked at my lap. I had shavings of ash from the fire that had spurted into the air and landed on my belly where I could not blow them off; they were pasted on by sweat, like small pieces of foam and plastic bits from a shattered snow globe. St. Lazarus had no inkling of the fact that by no means would I take sexually of this poor forgotten goddess. "What do you plan to do to her, Matanza? Are you a pleasure monger?" He looked at me and began to belch out staccato laughter. He was placing the sticks from the tree of all things around the fire pit. When he bent down, I heard his spine crack like a zipper being drawn down slowly. "Soon, boy, soon, we must converse, and you must move me with song. Then take your reward and dive into the most unfathomable depths of the deep briny drink. There you will find her, lying on a bed of abalone shells, chained to the coral, where you must become a man."

I looked up, right into St. Lazarus' manic face, his eyes darting from flame to flame. He was quiet. He held the bottle of rum between his outstretched legs. I could see the small rotten piece of Aphrodite's heart at the bottom, covered in a milky film that separated off the rum-preserved organ when the bottle shook. "Lazarus," I said, staring at the glass bottle. "Can you spare a cigarette?"

He looked up at me and smiled. "Ha, boy! You wish to burn one down?" he said, laughing.

"No, my man, I just wanted to start a dialog." I smiled and chuckled out a few lines. "I just wanted a real conversation, my old friend." I mimicked his posture by lying back supported by my elbows, then I rolled my eyes quizzically and blew a stray brown curl off my forehead. I have heard that mimicking posture makes your adversary more comfortable. It is part of my brinkmanship. My game theory.

He reached into the folds of his robe and pulled out a bent and crumpled cigarette. The cigarette had the words *Death's Head* printed around the filter. St. Lazarus picked up an ember with his bare fingers, the coal searing his skin with a loud sizzling sound like pork fat melting in a skillet. It smelled like burning hair. I placed the end of the cigarette in between my pursed lips and brought my face close to his burning fingers.

Grabbing his enormous hand with both of mine, I steadied the coal and inhaled deeply, lighting the butt. St. Lazarus' wrist was as thick and strong and fibrous as a horse's shin bone and had the approximate sinew.

I sucked the cigarette down. "Thanks, brew. You didn't have to give me a cigarette. I was only looking for a path into our required conversation," I said as I began to feel a copious amount of nicotine enter my lungs, then become absorbed by my alveoli, then enter my bloodstream, and then immediately attach to the dopamine receptors in my brain. I looked up at Lazarus with a head heavy and light at the same time. My neck felt like a loose uncoiling spring. My head rolled side to side as I tried to stabilize my vision. Electric currents were pulsating through my body with each dying heartbeat. The hair on the back of my neck and head stood up. I sat up and put my head in my hands, somehow withstanding the intense urge to vomit. I was sweating red water, like a hippo. "Dammit, I'm dying!" I exclaimed as I fought the urge of panic and pandemonium from this demon tobacco. St. Lazarus looked at me and began to laugh. He squashed the ember he still held in his fingertips. "How I would love to dip these seared fingers into a baptismal basin." He somehow said while he whistled a child's lullaby. "How could you be whistling as I am sitting here with my head in my hands about to die!" I yelled with what energy I had left after battling the effects of the Death's Head cigarette.

"Ring around the rosy, pocket full of posies, ashes, ashes, we all fall down. Ha!" He beamed as he belted out the old song. "You are not going to die," he bellowed, spurting words in a sporadic manner betwixt outbursts of gregarious laughter. "I must say that you are strong, Matanza! Be proud, for that cigarette can kill most living things within seconds!" St. Lazarus looked at me intensely and pressed his nine-inch-long index finger upon his lips. He was signaling me to be quiet. I leaned in amid gasps for air, fighting my body's want to lose consciousness. He guided my head towards his and placed my forehead on his forehead. He whispered directly into my face, his breath smelling like canned cat food and spoiled fruit salad. "Tigermother," he said as he licked his chapped lips with a smacking sound. Drops of saliva shot onto my face. "What's up, man?"

"I need something to drink, I'm not doing well," I said as I forced my numb arm to my face to wipe it off. St. Lazarus stared at my face; his breath unbearable.

"I wanted to see if you would die," he whispered into my mouth. "I honestly did not think that you would survive a Death's Head cigarette!" He began to laugh a wicked laughter, obscene and almost violent. "Oh, boy, but you are strong! You are very strong!"

I looked up at his face. His eyes resembled big, round, hard-boiled eggs with small bottomless pupils and tiny red veins drawn upon them. "You are evil," I said as I pushed him away and lay on my back. My world was still spinning, but I was not dead, and that was a good thing. The crickets were popping in and out of the sea grass around my head. The fire crackled like a bright and loud oriental celebration, the kind where ten-legged paper dragons rule the streets, jumping, dancing, menacing children, and hanging paper lanterns illuminate the people, giving them a warm green and red touch to their faces, softening the collective bevy's features in contrast to the sharp darkness of the Chinese night. The backside of the moon flickered behind the long bending leaves of the palm tree, making strange shadows and shapes on the soft sand, as if putting on a twisting and anamorphic shadow puppet show. Shapes and shadows became many things with the bend of a palm leaf or a breeze of the now-living wind. They then twisted into other things and states of mind and abstract concepts. An eagle became a bat, then turned into a fish, and finally the shadow became a deep sadness and longing. Here shadows could be feelings. They were moving me to feel again.

My heartbeat was deep and thunderous. It filled my ears. I could feel it throb in my neck. The garden hose veins in my forearms pulsated as if blood were being forced tumultuously through them by a series of industrial vacuums and gargantuan electrical pumps. With each beat my eyelids became heavier and heavier. They closed of their own accord. I did not will them to close. I wished to see what play the shadows would put on next. I wish they had shown me my origin story. Maybe they could have spelled my histories out in the sand with fluctuating light, punctuating my story with dark and obscure apparitions, foggy, almost imaginary, ghostly images of whispers of shadows. I thought of being, or more so, the mass of atoms that I was: my existence. I thought I had reached an unheard-of apex here, for my heartbeat was strong. Yet my apparent good will masked a deep inertia of coarse self-loathing. I had become the consummate form of indecorousness, the apotheosis of vulgarity.

The fire and cross-circuiting winds and palm leaves shifting and crickets and waves busting open onto the beach began to saturate and overstimulate my sensory receptors. Each sound would surprise me, shock me, and frighten me. At one point the waves sounded like a lion roaring, and I could hear the chatter of people hidden inside the shuffling of the palm tree. Yet these were not auditory hallucinations. They were my own ideas, thoughts, fears, and desires being imposed upon the voluptuous nature of the sounds of this place. I thought I heard my love whispering. I thought I heard a baby cry. I thought I heard a portable typewriter clicking away. Finally, a ding! I thought the mystery typist had finished his phrase. It was Roscoe banging the rum bottle with a tin can we used as a cup.

"Open your eyes, Matanza! It's time for rum." I sat up and opened my eyes slowly. St. Lazarus passed me the bottle of rum, reaching mischievously across the fire to where I was lying back. "Here, boy, drink." His outstretched brown arm bowed at the elbow over the fire so as not to get burned by the flames. He seemed to contort his body as if he were composed of putty and resin. I would not have been surprised to see drops of him melting off. The bottle's neck had virtually disappeared within his dark fist, and his rawhide knuckles were turning white from the strength of his grip.

I took the bottle and held it up close to my eyes and examined Aphrodite's heart closely for the first time. To my amazement, it was not a *piece* of her heart at all. This bottle contained her whole heart. But my entire concept of the heart was tossed asunder. For the heart itself was very, very, very small. It was about the size of a ripe cherry, the size of a newborn's heart, completely intact. I could see in all the possible scope of its detail—and its glory—that it was very beautiful, and it moved my eyes to well up with tears for the first time since living with St. Lazarus. Aphrodite must have been very dainty and small. Maybe she wore beautiful cloaks and robes made from woven strands of silken spiderwebs. Maybe her feet had been adorned with shoes made from hummingbird eggshells.

"She must have been tiny, almost wonderfully nymphean," I said as I held the bottle by its neck and stuck my index finger into its mouth, cleaning out the dead skin left behind from St. Lazarus' chapped lips that had accumulated over time.

"Ah, son, yes she was, for she had to be in order to quietly sneak into men's hearts and inspire their perversion and lust."

I looked up at St. Lazarus. "She stood for love, my man, all that is great in this world," I said as I put the bottle to my lips and took a small swallow. Aside from the perturbing stench, it was good rum—smooth, sweet, and mellow—one could taste the freshly cut sugar cane used carefully in its distillation. St. Lazarus must have been diligent in his handling of the liquor. He must have toiled greatly when refining this potent spirit. It must have been aged over centuries. I took another drink and he saw that I was enjoying it.

"You know, Matanza, it has been said that if you are able to finish the bottle in one large gulp and the piece of heart touches your lips, you will have good fortune. Ha, boy! You will need it from tonight on!"

St. Lazarus sat up. His ceremonial robe enveloped his body against the flickering firelight. The paint on his face had begun to fissure and show small cracks. The sections of paint were beginning to dry and separate. They moved slowly across his sweaty visage like the great sheets of ice that roam the ocean in the frozen northlands. His teeth and the whites of his eyes reflected an olive green and yellow against the white paint of the skull on his lower face. The rising sun on his forehead had begun to drip down in red specks. It looked as though someone had peppered his misshapen face with double odd buck shot. He grabbed his chin and the back of his head and tore his neck to one side violently, alleviating tension. It sounded as if one were snapping a pine board. "Ah, young Matanza, have you had your fill of rum?" He smiled as he pulled another Death's Head cigarette out of a black pack hidden in his robe. The cigarette was bent and almost broken. He put it in his mouth and stuck his entire face into the flames to light it. The tips of his nappy, white, salt-crusted hair and fatuously long eyebrows burnt off in the fire. He sat back again and finished the whole butt in one enormous drag. His inhale sounded like an asthmatic broken bagpipe heaving and sucking wind. The cigarette crackled. When he exhaled the smoke, he blew all kinds of patterns—Euclidean geometry— and shapes into the air. Not just rings of smoke, he blew parallelograms, rhombuses, trapezoids, even a crystal-clear spiral, a ghostly image of what seemed to be a transparent nautilus shell, that must have been the most accurate imitation of the logarithmic sequence I've ever seen, a Phidian spiral: $ED/DC = DC/CB = CB/BA$[23]. Near perfection. It glistened, translucent against the back of the moon. Forty-two smoky shapes in all hung above our heads. The breeze could not blow

---

[23] The Author is also a film photographer. His work is usually framed in city streets without the presence of people. He bases his work on the idea of intersecting lines, depth of field, curves and angles, and flatness as well actually. He is working from memory with this formula. He has the book in his possession. It was part of his study in undergraduate readings. But he is hoping, and committing to his memory, that he has remembered this formula correctly. Please advise if he has made an error.

them away. The figures were made from thick dense smoke which held its shape.

St. Lazarus stood awkwardly, shifting his weight around like an off-balance inebriate. Rubbing his hands together, he resembled a shamanic voodooist preparing a curse. Suddenly, he jumped up, and with one gigantic swat of his cyclopean hand sent every single one of the forty-two ghostly forms into history, destroying his unholy magnum opus. As soon as they disappeared, they were gone from my mind, as if I had sipped water from the Lethe. He looked down upon me since I was still sitting. "Furthermore, Matanza, you have not sloshed enough rum."

I looked up at him. "Lazarus, you cannot start a conversation with the word furthermore! You haven't talked since you lit your cigarette. I mean it's not proper," I snapped.

St. Lazarus wiped his face, leaving greasy paint streaks, and laughed into his hands. "Ah, boy, nothing is proper! Have you not learned that already? You who moved me by lying, by being selfish! It is perfectly acceptable in any vernacular to do what you wish. You told me that yourself. Please learn how to tell a good story!"

The moon whizzed and shook for a split second, like a buzzing button on a tilted, stalled pinball table. Or at least I thought it whizzed and shook. I wasn't sure anymore. I ran my fingers through my curls and puffed my dry hair up, deep in thought about lies, hallucinations, treacherous parlor games, women, about padding my résumé at cocktail parties and lying to the common street girls and bar rats for a quick gobble. I never do those things, so why is he willing me to consider these evils? My face gave my thoughts away. "Do not lament yourself over tearing your heart into morsels, boy. Banishment of your breath of life will make you so strong, a successful storyteller. You cannot tell a story about sex if you have never had it, right, Matanza?" piped St. Lazarus bellicosely as he squatted down to my size. His boney knees level with his face, as his bottom ever so gracefully hovered sheer millimeters from the sand.

He moved in closer to me and cupped my chin with his big palm, his long fingers grabbing and pressing in my cheeks. My jaw was squared up and my mouth felt pinched like fish lips. Surprisingly, his hand was not as coarse as I'd imagined. It felt like I was being held by the smooth palm of a giant newborn baby gorilla. He looked at me. "Matanza, reach into your pocket. Or have you forgotten?" I grabbed at his fist tightly holding my face and ripped it away. Grabbing the bottle of rum, I swilled down at least half. I was thirsty. I could feel the alcohol burning an ulcer in my stomach. A drop fell from the tip of the bottle as I took it from my lips and burned a smoking hole in my shorts. I wiped it off before it could blister and burn me.

"I don't want to be your friend. People I care for touch me, not you," I shouted with a modest temperament. St Lazarus jolted upwards and boomed laughter. He arched his back with his hands on his hips, his potbelly flopping up and down soporifically.

"Son!" He paused for a second like a machine gunner changing magazines. His laughter was like automatic fire. "You have nothing here but me!"

I realized he was right. He was the only thing I had here, besides the [her/him,] the duality of god in my dreams. I stood up and turned away from St. Lazarus, stroking the stubble on my chin, which was static and not growing into a beard. I paced from the fire and away from the rotting palm log. I looked out into the black ocean. There no stars to highlight the crests of the waves. I reached into my right pocket. My wrist got stuck at the opening, and the broad and braided seagrass bracelet got hooked against the pocket's rim. I fished its depths with the tips of my fingers, lightly grazing a wadded-up piece of paper. I was finally able to liberate it by using my index and ring fingers like weak pincers. Plucking it out of my palm, I realized it was the ribbon of the origami newspaper rose that was born of my lies. I opened it.

"SEDUCE PERSEPHONE, my man, that's what it says." St. Lazarus looked at me, smiling, his face like a joker on a worn-out deck of cards. I smiled back. His countenance was too amusing, preposterous, and grotesque to disregard.

"I'm afraid of what that could mean. I don't know what to think. Is Persephone a word? A person? For I only expect sorcerous bewilderment from you and your dark magic and this place's unearthly and unpropitious nature."

St. Lazarus began to play with his hair and coiled a thick chunk of it around his finger. He popped his digit free, and a long spongy curl was left stiff and hard against the rest of his hair. He was thinking. "Ah, young Matanza. What was born of your lies and your stories is for you to know!" He began to chuckle again, stopped abruptly, and continued his diatribe. "I know nothing but this: as secretive as this place makes me, I can only surmise that there is but a single truth here, and that the truth in question is you, tiny Matanza, and the storyteller you must become." I grabbed at my hair in frustration. Maybe

I was truth. Maybe I must learn how to exist as truth and somehow lecherously dally and philander with the mother ocean. What a devious crossroads! St. Lazarus cleared his throat loudly and spat a phlegm oyster the size of a fried egg onto the rotting palm log. "Matanza," he said softly since he was still gargling phlegm. "Perhaps Persephone is the greatest of all concepts. Perhaps Persephone is the most noble of all ideals. Perhaps Persephone was born the moment your lies forced the grand feminine of the soil to burst open with the lovely paper rose. Perhaps Persephone is a woman somewhere far away; perhaps she is nearby. Perhaps she is your salvation."

I could not wrap my head around the immense possibilities. I thought about Persephone as being a concept or a noble ideal. "Lazarus," I said as I kicked sand pensively and crossed my arms. "In my heart I know that truth only exists in the ideal, in what I consider real."

He gazed at me. The motions of his pupils were dizzying. "Son, in your heart you know nothing. You are nothing. You must be selfish and rapacious in your underhandedness regarding this situation." I forgot that St. Lazarus was unaware that my heart had begun to beat. He hadn't noticed yet. "My man, if Persephone exists here, with us, she would only be an imitation, a lie and falsehood. The seduction of an untruth would be the biggest lie of all." St. Lazarus stuck his hand out and touched my chest. His fingers were transferring a high-pitched frequency like supersonic vibrations. The energy was scaring me. "This boy does not exist," he said as he poked the skin above my heart. He poked me harder. "You must inhale the smoke from the tree of all things and become the slayer of your own soul." I stepped back from him since his incessant prodding was sharp and painful. "Matanza, you must be opaque. Show movement, but do not show them your intentions. Mislead others through lies and trickery, and always believe your contradictions. Whatever Persephone may be, she may impact you greatly."

I suddenly felt the urge to be gone from this place. To embrace my them. To feel their soft skin and place my head upon their single breast and be lulled to sleep by the delicate throbs of their humanity, ticking deep within them. I wished to ask their permission to slowly consume their heart kiss by kiss, piece by piece. Thoughts of them came in flickers: lightning. For a few moments, my passions and sufferings with them would make my head hot and sick. Then they would be gone again, my skull and spine numbed by this devil's many tongues. The real fear that gripped me was that St. Lazarus' words were becoming more and more understandable. He was slowly and mathematically plucking and pressing the correct sequence of knobs and buttons, introducing me to a world of wickedness and storytelling. I fought on, steadying my gelatinous spirit. Yet the brave action was almost impossible, for by this time I had become extremely drunk. The rum had made me susceptible to his rhetoric.

I could not seem to make my cortex function; speech was impossible. I muttered and gabbled like a turkey. I was stepping on my own toes, bobbing and weaving, crunching on ridiculously immense fishbones. I stumbled backward and fell, tripping over the palm log, banging my head viciously on the compacted sand. I looked a rotting fish head in the eye. St.

Lazarus' throat oyster was clinging to my fingers. I'd made the misstep of grabbing for the palm log as I fell.

"This is horrendous," I managed to stammer out as the breath of life from my exhalations, belches, and disgorges began to light up into blue flames from the alcoholic vapors catching fire. With each small burst of conflagration, a small amount of wind was sucked from my lungs, leaving me, for a small moment, breathless, like a careless person opening a window in an apartment that is ablaze.

St. Lazarus crept slyly over to me, slapping my face with the heavy end of a branch from the tree of all things. "Composure, son, composure." He took a deep breath and looked me over roughly, licking his palm with his broad, dog-like tongue. He wiped the sand and dirt off my face as if I were a small child. "Stability when sozzled, gassed, and over-lubricated is the uttermost, supreme, and most paramount ability a man can attain. Look at all the great men of any age, Matanza, they all had bloated and veiny red noses and pockmarks on their faces; they all kept their vice tightly against their chest in little pewter bottles, hidden in their garment's pockets; they all used women and lied. You, boy, cannot even begin to handle your rotgut," St. Lazarus said with a slightly depraved and iniquitous smile.

I wiped his viscous and mucilaginous phlegm onto my pants. It stuck so thick that it webbed my fingers together. Thick strings, brown and yellow and heavy, dripped from my palm. Its odor was strong enough for me to taste the salty curd. I could feel the rum come back into my gullet, my stomach contracted in a steady cadence, its own special rhythm. It could have been a 5/4, each downbeat pushing the foamy heave slowly towards my mouth.

"Son!" he burped out like a bullfrog with a punctured throat. "Do not dare let yourself evacuate the rum from your bowels. For it is not only rum that you have spilled down your craw, but also Aphrodite's debauched humanity!" St. Lazarus wound up hard and punched me straight in the gut. The pain seemed unendurable but only lasted for a blinding moment. My eyes bulged as if I were in a faulty decompression chamber. My tongue shot straight out. My body re-ordered its shameful priorities, and I swallowed down the heaving mass. His blow had syncopated the meter of my throbbing insides and the song had begun to quiet down.

I smartly and quickly began to envision a different scenario. This stagnation was puzzling me. I wanted good fortune. I desperately needed a break from the monotone, the shrill laughter, the menacing stares, and St. Lazarus' continuous assaults on my developing manhood and heart. "My man," I said as I pounded my diaphragm repeatedly, hoping to calm the uproar deep in my venter. "You said that if Aphrodite's heart touches my lips in one enormous gulp that I shall be granted good fortune?"

He looked me dead in the eyes and, with an ominous grin, chuckled and shook his head from side to side. "Son," he said as he moved in closer. I could still see the imprint left by his mammoth fist dented into my midsection. "Son," he repeated, "if by any chance you were to evacuate the remaining volume of this boof into your belly pouch, a poisoning of grand and immense proportions would follow you. No man I have seen has had the gumption and exquisite fierceness to finish off this bottle." My mind meandered through the words St. Lazarus had just spoken, a warning of sorts. But I saw the flower of possibilities outweigh the risks. To submit myself to the burning pain of this godless spoiled drink and purse my lips to kiss Aphrodite's rotten heart and dialog in the patois of the gods and reach an apex of good fortune seemed like a risk worth the effort of a chthonic death.

I steadied my bruised, drunk, and sick body. I forced the strength from my core to stand. The fire cast waves of shadows across my frame, playing with my features; for a moment my body became subdued, defined sharply by the transient light. I raised my right arm and opened my hand. "Lazarus," I said, my hair soaked in sweat, covering my eyes and half my face, "pass me the bottle, for I plan the unthinkable."

He had the look of a delighted child spread across his gleaming facial features. "Ah, son, so you opt for what is not in your best of best interests. A terrible idea, I think, but brave you must be, now that you have come this far." He walked towards me and passed me the bottle from underneath his robes. It glimmered like worn sea glass against the shadows of the flames. The stench made my belly quiver and tremble once more. I took a long look at the heart inside, brown and covered in a mist of milky white film. I pinched my nose and swallowed down the liquor in one painfully enormous gulp. I felt a soft, tender, and beautiful kiss upon my pursed lips at its end when the heart touched my mouth. It was as though I had kissed once more a lover I used to know. The wind howled and whipped the embers of the fire bright like shimmering gold upon the sand. It stirred my heart and moved me, for I had not been poisoned at all; I was alive, and as I focused my extremely rum-drunken eyes on the murky glass bottle I began to hear a slight tip-tapping sound against the glass. I wondered at this quaint curiosity. "What have I done?" I asked myself. I spat on the side of the bottle and polished it against my shorts. Then I realized upon a deeper examination that Aphrodite's rotten heart had turned a deep cherry red and had begun to beat again.

I collapsed into a drunken exhaustion. Fragments of fractions of memories began to flood my mind. I could not find the face of anything within the sharp and tiny shards that brought me an unwanted surprise. The firelight seemed brighter than the dying sun at the crispest of autumn sunsets. The crackles of the wood in the fire seemed to boom and echo like cannon fire into solid oak planks of a tall-masted man of war. Splinters of sparks were shot onto my skin, and I was drowning in immensely sharp bursts of burning pain. My senses had been heightened by the enormity of my intoxication; the dying embers too intense to look at directly. The sweat from my brow was burning my eyes, as if I were being forced to accept drop after drop of pure capsaicin onto my iris, permeating my entire ocular cavity. I moaned in searing agony. I had liberated Aphrodite's heart from its slumber, but the price that I was paying was as steep as the most grueling and treacherous climb up onto the highest Andean plateau. I regained my composure for a fraction of a second and almost stumbled into the blazing fire. I jumped around St. Lazarus, who at this point must have believed my death was inevitable. I gathered my failing strength and threw the bottle against the thickest of the fishbones on the sandy ground, smashing the glass. Reaching down into the shards and pale sand, I pulled out Aphrodite's beating heart, blew it clean, and put it into my pocket. I could feel the strong tip-tapping thud it made against my thigh.

"Whoo-hoo-hoo!" yelled St. Lazarus as he shuffled over, crouching slowly towards me, blowing thick gray smoke from his nostrils, propping his head on his rubbery neck sideways, glaring into my face as I looked vacantly into the lapping flames, as if in a trance. I stood with my belly facing the fire, my body's musculature looked very defined against the bright firelight as I looked myself over. The light and heat had reached a crescendo, a crown, almost a culmination; it was like the fire had become an enormous red dwarf consuming its surroundings as if we were the solar system and the largest gas planets: I was Jupiter. "Are you dead, son?" he asked with a fat-lipped, puckered grin, shuffling his lips against his teeth. I could hear his cracked lips grind against his bare dry gums and cracked enamel. It sounded as if someone were polishing a tin can with steel wool. "Are you dead, dying, indisposed, pushing up the daisies, son?" St. Lazarus asked jokingly, gesticulating wildly with his powerfully long fingers, in between shot gun blasts of offensive laughter.

"No," I said as I wobbled like a rum pot bibber and a cheap plastic bobble-head doll. My balance seemed to have been adversely affected by the supremely stiff, roaring swill-bowl I had just downed. I looked up at him and began to laugh, clutching my ribs since the bomb of the booze was burning my insides as I shook. "I'm just drunk, man, just wicked hammered!" I said, laughing out loud with a deep sense of relief since I had survived the barbarously poisonous levels of intoxication.

After composing myself, I paced rapidly towards the sea. I could hear St. Lazarus yell from the fire pit, "So you stole for yourself that wench's dirty tiny little heart, a keepsake for your grand efforts." He laughed in quick measured breaths as I managed to make my way to the side of the ocean without tripping over old tin cans, rum bottles, or fishbones. "I was a-hoping it would be your end!" he said smirking. I could see his rotten teeth from the beach. I must have been quick when I grabbed the tiny organ, for St. Lazarus did not see the pulsing of my right-side pocket. He had not noticed that Aphrodite's heart was once again beating, and for some reason, I had been the one to liberate pure love from its slumber. The moon had turned to see me as it had not done so before; I could see its cratered and pockmarked face in the dead and starless night sky. St. Lazarus again yelled from the fire pit as he danced around the flames, resembling a Dakota warrior bringing about the rain. He had a stick from the tree of all things, shaking it up and down in one hand; it was black against the firelight. "We must turn your soul to ash, young Matanza! And then, and then, you must move me with song before we must unbridle your rapacious nature against the harlot in the sea!"

I stepped into the tepid ocean, the waves busting over and tapping my toes as if they were playing a thunderous and mellifluous, almost polyphonic symphony, using my small phalanges like the keys on a piano. The wind was racing across my sweaty form as I dipped down and scooped up water to wet my face and head. My woven grass bracelet soaked up water like a sponge. I could feel it loosen against my wrist. I could hear the edges of the palm leaves on the trees whistle as they cut through the air. I could hear the dying fire roar as the wind erupted through the flames, feeding the embers with pure oxygen, making the fire reach two stories above the palm-frond hut. The wind was back at my side again, and it was powerful. "Ah, son, do you feel it? The breeze is an angry one tonight, Matanza," St. Lazarus bellowed as he began to burn the tip of the branch from the tree of all things. He looked small and frail and old against the shadows cast by the now-vibrant moon and the firelight. His robes looked more tattered and ancient than they did ceremonial and prodigious. The palm-frond hut looked like a ramshackle dwelling from the poorest village in the third world. The sad, tall palm tree was bent and almost broken after withstanding the weight of one thousand nights like this one. It had seen too much of these things and the burden was beginning to snap at its once-strong fibrous core. I could understand what happened to its brother tree now rotting away as a log near the fire pit. St. Lazarus was beginning to look more and more like a poor and weak old man.

I turned my face away from the firelight and all its very dispirited trappings and looked out into the jet-black ocean, only able to see the gray tip tops of the burgeoning waves as they slowly reached the evolving shore. My hair, curled and wet, covered my face. I felt crazy reckless. Raising both my arms to my sides and with my feet together, I opened my hands and, resembling a crucified man, fell straight back, sacrificing myself upon the flat surf and sand. My head impacted painfully and bounced along the riptide. Alas, some pain was required for me to wake up from this dream, this strange and terrible dream. I tried to hold my breath while wincing at the sharp hurt at the back of my skull. Opening my eyes, I could see dark shadowed gray bubbles and hear the clamor, repercussion, and rebound of each impacting wave. The beautiful tumult filled my ears for what seemed like minutes and for a moment I lost track of my space. How beautiful to feel lost. I pursed my lips and shot my head upwards to draw in a deep breath. I could feel the cold breeze upon my exposed lips, and I was brought back down to realize that here I still lay in the outer islands, together with the wind, drunk, with a beating heart in my pocket, and here with the unholy Lazarus, a racking and afflictive bad influence.

I lay motionless on the undulating sea currents, wondering if it was at all possible to make my bed here and fall asleep while floating on the waves. I realized the impossibility of my thought and with deep intent began to petition both the wind and the one with no name. Grabbing a handful of wet sand, I raised my left arm from the water and a sharp gust blew each granule of sand, one by one, up into the caliginous and murky night sky. I said my thanks for my strength and wished my soul would never turn to ash. Remembering the small treasure I carried upon me, I reached into my pocket and with my thumb and forefinger gently pressed the seat and center of Aphrodite's secret thoughts and emotions. I suddenly felt a profound sense of warmth slowly caress the tips of my fingers and move resplendently up my arm and through my chest until it had deluged the entirety of my essence and existence. I now knew this place was real, for a feeling of such depth and wholeness cannot exist as an untruth. I knew now that I could move forward without fear. In love there resides great strength.

I stood up slowly, not wanting to leave the ocean or these new warm feelings and turned towards the palm-frond hut. With complete ease of mind, I navigated the minefield of trash, tin cans, fishbones, and other obstacles without even glancing at my feet. It was as if I were gliding on top of a cumulonimbus cloud, being held up by cracking shards of lighting. I made my way back to the rotting palm log where St. Lazarus sat tapping the end of a cigarette against the back of his hand, rather gracefully for a person of his objectionable and vulgar character. The fluidity of his movements surprised me. "Even the most undesirable of people are allowed to have some semblance of elegance," I thought.

"Lazarus, I'm going back into the ocean, this time deep where the big fish are, 'I am quite drunk, I want to meet the goddess of the sea." I stumbled up and jumped over fishbones and tin cans, ran headlong into the sea, and dove as deep as I could with one enormous breath until I began to sink into the dark oblivion.

Los Dialogos del Diablo

Recitative

Jolene, the lover of language and legends

6

Down in the deep water, the murk and mire of ancient people's histories, buildings and cities that have been covered in ocean currents and forests of kelp, homes and hearths from Atlantis, old plowed fields, hills, and fertile lands that now are the home of fishes and great beasts that sailors fear, hovering underwater near their ships, spouting spray as tall as Lebanese cedars, bucking and beating against their wooden ships, causing some men to panic, others to stoutly board a dinghy and harpoon the creatures and take their bodies aboard. That is where I found the old wisdom and the goddess of the sea. Under the foam of the spray and waves—which are Neptune's horses racing against the shore—deep in the blue water where bubbles from my breath squeezed out from my mouth like soapy little dreams that we forget after we arise from sleep. Deep down near a bunch of coral where clownfish and pufferfish bumped into my legs, and the tentacles of anemones stung when I touched them with my outstretched fingers, and jellyfish randomly danced and were thrown into my way like floating debris on a blustery autumn day, I saw a plastic milk crate that had a square of plywood placed over its top with a large rock holding it down. Fastened to the plywood with tin buckles was a small chalkboard with an eraser and piece of yellow chalk tied to its corner with brown hemp twine. The chalkboard had the phrase "It's all actually quite absurdly simple when it's explained to you" written in beautiful Spenserian penmanship, the word "you" written in a gorgeous and flowing copperplate calligraphy, and under the phrase it was signed with the name "Jolene Armitage."

I lifted the heavy porous black rock off the plywood and slowly and cautiously peered under the board, expecting something to jump at me, like those terrifying jack-in-the-boxes that scare the absolute shit out of children. Removing the plywood, I saw in the milk crate an old pin-up illustration of a 1950s American diner waitress serving a cup of coffee, a box of yellow chalk, a few seashells, and a small green bottle that was worn over entirely like sea glass and had a yellowed paper tag labeling it as "strong medicine." There was an old and rusted opinel #8 pocketknife, which was dulled from shucking oysters, and next to that was what looked like a tennis ball, but on further inspection was only a ball made from multiple elastic bands wrapped around each other.

I took up the chalkboard and erased Jolene's message. Grabbing the small bit of yellow chalk, I wrote the following words: "Dearest Jolene, my name is Señor Matanza. Having no want to fornicate with the ocean, I find myself wondering what I should do, and I am only looking to have a chat, so if you could explain things to me so I can understand my position plainly and with absolute clarity I would be most appreciative. I believe I have found you at the bottom of the sea and from all quarters[24] have listened to your story.[25] Cheers and warm regards, Señor Matanza." To my astonishment, my words disappeared from the chalkboard, and again "It's all actually quite absurdly simple when it's explained to you" began to slowly emerge from the slate of the board in yellow chalk. This time it was followed by the valediction "Your little buddy, Jolene Armitage."

"There is something detestable when men are discourteous to their verbs, especially men who you hope one day to fuck. 'From all quarters have listened to your story'? Really?" I heard whispered very faintly as if someone was letting air escape from a balloon a few yards away.

"Hello?" I asked quizzically, wondering where this voice was coming from.

"I said you are incredibly discourteous to language, Señor Matanza, and it is very unbecoming." I still had very little idea of where this voice came from and to whom it belonged, and I was getting upset that it was questioning my use of grammar.

"Okay. Hold on." I looked around nervously. The water made everything look like the horizon at the edge of a hot desert. "Firstly," I said, "I am in no way interested in any

[24] . "Quarters," referring to the older English usage of "person" or "places."
[25] . This was improvised from "A Scandal in Bohemia." An unknown correspondent writes in a letter, on a paper that is "peculiarly strong and stiff," asking Sherlock Holmes for a private interview. "We have from all quarters received," is meant to show that colleauges have spoken highly of Sherlock. Holmes deduced that the man who wrote the letter is German due to his treatment of English verbs. He confirms this by searching his "Continental Gazetteer," after identifying the watermark on the letter, and noting that the author comes from a place renown for its glassmaking and paper mills.

113

philandering and getting weird at the bottom the ocean. Secondly, I don't like when strange voices whisper criticism of my use of language, and thirdly, where are you so I can at least see what I am talking to?" I heard nothing in response except for the tumult of a storm miles above me, rocking the surface of the ocean, churning the blue depths and swaying me from side to side as I floated a few feet from the bottom of the sea.

"I know you are Señor Matanza."

"That I am," said I, still curious as to who was addressing me.

"You can call me Jolene. I live here in the milk crate, next to the bottle, penknife, the elastic band ball, and the pin-up of the waitress. The sky was my husband, and I gave birth to most everything in the world." I wondered what had happened between her and the sky. Relationships are so odd, I thought, especially ones that last for an eternity.

"I know the wind," I said, since I knew really nobody here. "I know St. Lazarus, and I saw Them in my dreams." I heard a deep laughter come from the milk crate, still airy and held together by hissing whispers.

"They all know nothing of you," said she mockingly. "You were a tiger," said Jolene Armitage. I could hear a sadness in her voice, a dip into the melancholy minor chords people make when thoughts of longing cross their minds at the moment of speaking.

"Me, a tiger?" said I, unsure as to what she meant.

"You were a foul thing, a disease, a curse to those who cared for you, an unrelenting indefatigable thing, a mass that existed to cause pain." I was shocked at having heard this about myself, for I knew nothing of my histories or loves or loss or lives or longing. I almost apologized as her metallic voice trailed off in a short, throaty, raspy hiss.

"I know nothing of those things," I said as I pulled my shorts back to my hips since they were being pulled off by the strong tides.

"You are here now, with us, so there is no use in questioning how, only in questioning 'why.' We must question the 'why,'" said Jolene quietly, as I struggled to hear her since her voice trailed off like the remnants of a nap-time dream. "There is a realm where most men and women are taken out of their expertise, and that is love, lies, and language. Are we all not either fucking or fighting? It's the same everywhere, in every land, in every culture. Nobody understands themselves enough to understand love and language. It's true. You can be a self-actualized go-getter, and the minute a foul passion strikes, all reason floats into the ether and we become pheromone-driven creatures of lust and blood and sour moods and sex that smells earthy, that musk that people's bodies breathe on each other, which sticks to one's fingers and mouth. But we have language. We are all brought together by language. That's what makes it powerful. Not the ability to destroy someone's ego, which in some cases is a great use of language, or the ability to bring an end to war through dialog, another great use of language, or even the ability to crystallize our most precious thoughts onto a printed page. No, the real power in language is to seduce; to persuade, to feign, and to strike at the root, the heart of another being. It's what makes us so powerful as people. The most seductive of all language is that of honesty. One does not seduce with lies; those are inexperienced fools who build themselves up. If you are awkward, seduce awkwardly; if you are kind, seduce with kindness; if you are a brute, then seduce with force. Language is as fluid as water, and as powerful. It can cut through stone, through hearts like stone, and drown out those dead wasted hearts. To master language as a human mother tongue—to be understood—regardless of what dialect we all speak, or our differences, is power. The only common diction is love, the only language we need is love, language is love, words are the beats of a heart, verbs, stative and dative, nouns, phrasal verbs, grammar parsing. A linguist is more alchemist and lover than anything else."

"Am I to understand that language holds the key to power?" I said quizzically.

"Señor Matanza, I need you to spend time with me," said Jolene in a whisper as I ran my fingers through my curly hair, which was being swayed by the tides above me. I wondered how St. Lazarus fornicated with her since she was only a series of letters on a chalkboard and knickknacks inside of a milk crate, yet this seemed like a place of deep magic that I did not understand.

"I could use a friend as well," said I in return. "I don't presume to understand anything about much," I said quizzically. "But I think that having a friend is sometimes okay. I think I may be a loner, but I'm not sure."

She laughed at me and it sounded like bubbling air escaping from a leaky basketball. "You have never known love, that I can say. I know of you and don't love you, the her/him may love you or may not, who knows, but you come from a vacuum of love, you do not speak the language, nor can you ever."

I looked at the milk crate since I could not look at any face and thought out loud. "I am not one to speak in riddles. I seem too plain to understand the illustrations on a printed page. I seem to not be able to find meaning in anything really but dreams. I seem only to exist. In no way do I feel any emotion. I can't find meaning," I said, more to myself than to her. I was only putting my theories into words. "You can only find meaning in language, that which goes said, and unsaid, that is what illuminates meaning." I sat crossed legged floating in the depth, curious as to language and asking myself if I could truly even speak.

"You have to learn how to tell stories." Said Jolene as the currents rocked me up and over, and kelp was thrown into my open mouth.

I heard a hiss and a whisper, a few deep aluminum-type robotic breaths, and Jolene softly said, "Señor Matanza, tell me a story, tell me something about yourself."

I thought as I floated and bubbles and wisps of current swayed over and around me, and I wondered, since I knew nothing of my history, what kind of story I could tell. "Jolene, I don't know anything about myself, except that I was a tiger, or an animal of some kind."

The milk crate fell over on its side, rolled by a deep current wave, and Jolene said, "You were the Tigermother, a matriarch of the beasts in the jungle, unloved and unloving of most, incapable of love, a pariah. Now tell me about the first time your murdered someone." Having no recollection of such an event, I wondered what I would have to say. The hiss and metallic voice roared back and said, "If you know nothing of yourself, just invent it, make it up, and what you say will become the truth."

"If it were to become true then I should think greatly about what language I will use," said I as I pondered what to make up.

"No, Señor Matanza, don't think too much. Language is truth. Uttering anything nowadays makes it truth in this post-truth world, so invent something and become it."

I swam down to the craggy rocks where the chalkboard was and began to freely invent a narrative of my life. I picked up the chalk and wrote the following words: "What troubles this place, old man?" I heard those words over and over in my head. Those were the words I said to the first man I murdered when I was thirteen. He had a fat double chin and his jowls hung dolorously from his purple lips that were always wet with spittle. He rarely took exercise and always snorted a pinch of snuff from a silver case with a beryl and pearl lid when it rained buckets on sunny days. He was terrified of dying. I remember he would walk around the center of town always saying, 'It's raining on a sunny day! The devil is getting married!' I heard he was a terrible boy, inflicting pain on animals, and once when he was a young awkward man, he pushed a young novitiate nun to the ground in between a pharmacy and a vacant lot, near the school where she worked, and molested her, sticking his chubby fingers far into her body and marveling at the wetness, recoiling in disgust afterwards, since he would never again feel a woman's warmth, or moistness, or love. He dedicated his life to becoming an archivist at a local university branch office, learning the secrets behind the planning of every metropolitan capital in Europe and the Americas, trying to figure out why architects let their plans get ruined by engineers, always stifling their creativity: 'If money wasn't an option, and we all had a true and honest say on our personal property, I say to you all that I could, and would, design a home so infinitely small and tiny, yet stately and grand and opulent, that all of the estancieros in Argentina would respect me!' he yelled, pointing an angry finger in the air one day at a city planning meeting where he felt a curious and unsettling attraction to the young mustached clerk taking the minutes of the meeting, scratching illegible notes in writhing agony as he valiantly and silently battled a rough and bloody case of hemorrhoids.

After a few minutes of silence, the words shifted and danced upon the slate like ghosts. I heard whispers of dead languages, the letters changed shapes and forms, a rhombus became a triangle, the triangle an eagle, and finally, a mathematically perfect cube bled into the form of the goat-headed Mephistopheles upon his throne, staff in hand, and was absorbed into the chalkboard. Jolene cried out in her tin-box voice, "Very good! You can turn a phrase! Now that language is your truth! Believe in it and it will be so."

I chuckled at Jolene's love of language and the absurdity of a conversation with a collection of odds and ends inside of a milk crate, but it made me happy to write. I enjoyed it.

"Now," Jolene said, "tell me a short tale of your past, where you grew up. It doesn't have to be much. We are just creating you from scratch. As long as you leave with a rough draft of who you were we can call today a success."

Now I knew nothing except for my her/him and the outer isles. I'd heard some tales of Persephone, but I knew nothing of where I grew up. I held onto a craggy coral rock as the water pushed and pulled from all directions, and the small minnows pecked at the dead skin on my calloused feet. "Do you want me to make it up?" I asked, wondering aloud.

"Yes," said Jolene, and the voice was almost unbearable due to the tumult of waves crashing overhead. "Invent your own odd truth, but it's the turn of the language that I love. Be creative and make me believe in the story, although some great works of prose have no story, and are just the anima of the composer on the page. Take it any way you like."

I again took up the chalk, this time in my left hand, since I wanted to train myself in being ambidextrous, and started to scrawl bits and pieces of a short history of mine that would become my truth. I slowly and tenuously wrote the following story, maybe from a memory or a dream I once had:

"It was far from anything at all normal—that is, the situation with Ezekiel Pantus. That's what I heard around town while I was getting a few bottles of fernet for the underage Bolivian kids who lived in the shanty slum town by the futbol field and artificial lake. Apparently, in an act of incredible bravery, or abject stupidity, he challenged the town drunk, who, by chance, was a distant relative of mine, and excellent company, to throw fists over the honor of a very slow-witted red-haired magazine vending girl, who he was infatuated with. Now, this whole situation could have been avoided. Nobody involved had even digressed from proper etiquette. However, Pantus mistook the town drunk, laying a two-peso banknote with his large thick brown fingers and fungus-eaten cuticles heavily and violently onto the boards of her kiosk as an act of impropriety. Ezekiel was the son of the head librarian, who gave him too many plainly written romance novels to read. On top of that, he thought that Sancho Panza was the most striking hero in Cervantes' monograph on chivalry, but the most curious thing about 'spaghetti-necked Pantus,' as the diabetic town priest called him, was his incredibly large, onion-shaped head. He once asked his mother as he cried over his Patoruzito comic books when he was only a small boy, why the children at school laughed at him and said that he was strange. 'Mama, do I really have a large head?' he asked in between sobs and foamy gargled grunts. His mother held him close to her, for she knew that this boy was kind and soft and rare like a curly-haired foal. She felt she had to raise a lovely little boy, her own little foppish dandy. 'Ezekiel, you are perfect," she said lovingly, holding back tears. "Now take your hat to the market and fill it with ten pounds of potatoes and a few onions for dinner.'"

Jolene leaked out a response like a punctured bike tire and said: "It has come to my attention that storytelling is a way into the heart of a woman. I want you to tell me stories, use language to seduce, and ideas, and grammar, and lexicon, and syntax. Some people say that literature is formulaic. I want you to break the formula of storytelling. Instead of suffering, make your protagonist only a vehicle to observe, have them tell the story through their eyes. Is conflict in three acts really what we should be aiming for? I want you to develop short paragraphs, short bits of stories that you can piece together with a turn of metrical sentences, a master sentence, polysyndeton, or metaphor, lay the conflict bare in what happens to the main actor's thoughts, for conflict can be internal as well as external. Try for a second, tell me a story. It could be true or bullshit. St.

Lazarus taught you how to bullshit, right? Regardless, it matters not, you are only here to have a conversation." She paused for a second. "Tell me a story in a paragraph, talk to me of legends and magic, an Arabian princess, for example. Entertain me, Señor Matanza," she said, sounding like she was speaking from the far end of a long hallway.

I took a breath and continued. "Many years ago, in 1883, during the French occupation of Tunisia, there was a homely but lovely young woman, who was the learned daughter of the Caliph, who fell in love with a legionnaire. She was a devout Muslim and a scholar of all the algebraic formulae and mathematical designs of Arabic antiquity; she would host interfaith dialogs with Imams, and Priests, and politicians. I heard that she developed a new school of progressivism in her branches of science and philosophy that are still studied by some esoteric scholars who blend music, religion, and science, but her voice was silenced by the patriarchy and she was banished to a far-away land and in exile wrote her most moving work, which was found only a few years ago hidden away, tucked inside the pages of an illuminated manuscript, dedicated to her legionnaire lover who perished mysteriously on the long journey trying to reunite himself with her after his lifetime of service in the legion."

I could hear a hissing laughter, as if a tea kettle were boiling over furiously. "There you go, Señor Matanza! That tale was only a paragraph long! Good. Do we really need to have a three-act play with conflict and anti-heroes and maidens fair and justice or the lack of it?"

I wondered aloud, "I may not be one who is graced creatively, but how does practicing learning storytelling as obtuse and short winded as this benefit me?"

Jolene gasped out some laughter, or should I say, I heard some distant laughter from everywhere all at once. "You must learn to tell short stories, because Persephone has a terrible attention span, and she needs a friend to tell her tales of love, passion, grace, and kindness. You will seduce her with your tales and truly honest thoughts, as short as they may be."

I sat crossed legged as the ocean currents pulled me far, then back near the milk crate and the baubles inside of it. "I don't want to seduce anyone," I said, thinking aloud.

"You can seduce most anyone into believing anything, or into feeling happy or sad. Stories that bring out emotion are all seductions of the most passionate. You, having felt no passion but bloodlust in your previous life, know nothing of this, so just think, think out loud, write things down, become Persephone's friend."

I thought that it would be lovely to have a good friend here. "Shall I try for another?" said I eagerly.

"Yes, and this time tell me a horror story in one paragraph."

Horror, how could you condense the narrative into a few sentences? I wracked my brain for a few minutes, stroking my chin. I thought of smoking a cigarette; however, fire doesn't work under the sea. I began thinking out loud again.

"Thirty years ago, but in a far-gone century, when I was only a boy, I was walking through the streets of London in the rain, and there I saw a brown leathery object lying in the grass. It was tufted at its base with what looked like pieces of rag and strips of velvety material, and it was rounded on its top. I saw, upon further inspection, that it was a human skull. To my surprise and incredulity, I realized I had chanced upon Oliver Cromwell's severed head. Now for those who don't know who Cromwell was, he happened to be the man who mobilized England's royalists and parliamentarians against each other. After winning the war he was appointed the Lord Protector of the Commonwealth. I took his head, which was severed under the direct orders of Charles the Second, and placed it upon my wooden mantelpiece, where it adorned my study for many years. As I grew madder year by year, from alcohol abuse, soliciting heavyset prostitutes for dinner dates, stealing rectal thermometers from hospitals and snorting the mercury inside on every month that ends in "R," and very liberally applying laudanum to my tobacco, I began to talk to Oliver's head, and we had many a marvelous chat by my fireside as we both sat on my Persian hearth rug and drank wine and told tales of old adventures. It was such a beautiful connection, one that will last forever, and not as solitary as it once was, since I have begun adding and collecting other heads to keep Oliver company as I prowl and roam the streets of London in the rain."

Jolene squeaked like a rusty wagon axle, laughing and taking in vacuum-like breaths. "Very good! I liked that one. It was quite slow in the beginning, but the last sentence was good, and the concept of making me think was paramount." I smiled at her approval. "Now tell me a story about awkward illicit love and tragedy. Do your best, you are only here to practice a little bit. Remember, seduction happens through the eyes, even in language, so help me see what you are saying." Jolene whispered the last part and I barely heard her.

"Hmm," I said out loud. "Awkward illicit love and tragedy, eh? I will do my best." I swam a few feet away from the milk crate and grabbed the pin-up poster of the diner waitress for inspiration and started to tell my story.

"Many years ago, I was working for a government agency, far from the middle of the pack—the middle having disappeared through anarchy on one side and dictatorship on the other. For me, education is of the highest regard and of the deepest moment, and I took with pride the things that I had accomplished. It so happened that I was planning a curriculum for those who have struggled to reach the shores of my country in peace, fleeing from war. It so happened on a hot May afternoon as I was assessing the development of my refugee students that, by chance, one of them was the most beautiful woman I had laid eyes upon. A woman of the tropics, dark-haired and blue-eyed. I made every possible overture while correcting her entrance exam to have her placed in my class. At sixteen, she was a vision of uncorrupted beauty, a doll with skin as nubile as porcelain and hands as expressive as the sunset on the deepest and most fathomless nights at sea. I loved her from afar for many months and wondered how a strange man like me could ever learn to appreciate such grace while she was surrounded by wolves. I watched to my horror as she was passed around the other members of the class, quietly and purposefully lending out sexual favors for friendship. I could not save her from her own choices, for each must learn their own pain and understand it; but how I wished to protect such a creature, such a kind-hearted girl from the darkest of South American nations, growing up humbly and virtuously on a farm, thrown into the tumbling and violent circus that most ravenous men hungry for virgin pussy tend to take part in, since they smell vulnerability like a fresh kill in the distance. It broke my heart to see her fumbling, yearning to understand herself, growing into adulthood, and making those choices that I saw with my age as volatile and full of self-loathing and the unendurable pain of self-knowledge."

"That story was disturbing," said Jolene in a thunderous whisper. "You have a talent for telling stories, and in time you will become a sage and wise scribe; but let me say that for us, all of us here who will benefit from your tales, do so only with honesty. As in grammar and syntax and style in writing, once one learns the rules, one can then break them and make great art. Once you hear your histories and learn of yourself, you will make your honest thoughts and not the narrative what drives the tales. And when you finally get to meet Persephone, don't lie to her; seduce her with your truth. Now, go and leave me to the fishes of the deep." I slowly backed away from the milk crate and the knife and bottle and chalkboard; as I went further away, I heard a loud hiss again.

"Señor Matanza, please pick up that picture of the diner waitress, fold it carefully along its edge, then fold it again along the crease, and carry it with you in your pocket always, and remember that you have a friend in the unknowable deep sea where the monsters swim and where, once before covered by floods, the fossils of beasts and fowl that roamed the Earth are with me always. I will remember you fondly surrounded by the bones of my children and the creatures that say hello on bright sunny days, darting through kelp and coral." And with that I swam back towards the surface of the sea and towards a beach unknown to me.

Persephone the Wise

7

There was a very sharp ringing sound followed by an incredible clanging noise and a droning buzz that could wake the entire neighborhood. On occasion it got very noisy for reasons nobody understood on the outer islands. It seemed to come from everywhere all at once. Persephone covered her ears and muttered things silently to herself to keep from going deaf. Her inner words and dialogs were muffled, and her head pounded as her blood pressure rose from the stress of the noise. The fish hag was nowhere to be seen, nor was the fishmonger, who must have been on one of his long trips into the deep ocean looking for the big fish. In her pocket she kept a small key that was attached to her belt loop with a small silver chain. She unlocked her cage with a snap and twist of the bolt and still covering her ears shot up out of the cage and ran as fast as she could towards the water, her small feel carving deep holes into the wet sand, each footprint filling with foamy water as she shot towards the ocean through the tides. Now you may wonder why she carries a key to her own cage. Well, Persephone is quite different; she enjoys being locked up in her tiny cage and tied down tight with hemp ropes that burn and leave marks on her body. She is torn between loathing the fishmonger and loving the uncomfortable pain he causes her when he ties her up and whips her with riding crops made from braided seagrass and when he places dozens of wooden clothespins around her pink nipples while the fish hag watches, eating rotting papayas and all kinds of strange and dripping tropical fruits. The noise suddenly stopped, and she meandered back to her cage and lay down to rest, that is until she saw a newcomer.

There was a curious-looking man standing, doing nothing, just looking in Persephone's direction. He seemed confused and out of place, curly-haired, somewhat thick for symmetry, and wore once-tan cargo shorts haphazardly clinging to his hips. He had a stubbly kind of beard, not long or unkempt, just one of those beards men have after not shaving for a few weeks. His mustache was a bit thicker than the rest of his facial hair. He was peering over the pots and kettles of the fish hag, fiddling with chains hanging them over the fire, muttering a few things to himself, and then starting to move towards Persephone's cage. He sauntered to and fro, looking a tiny bit wobbly; maybe he had had too much to drink. He ran one of his big hands—for they were larger than most men's—through his hair and tried a strange sort of side part, picking loose curls from his forehead.

Persephone noticed this strange newcomer and quickly unlocked her cage and stood up as alert as a meerkat, as fierce as a jaguar, yet peering at the new man with a kind of narrow-eyed mistrustful benevolence. "Hey!" she said as she marched towards him, swinging one arm, the other held akimbo, her hand upon her waist, as was her peculiar way of walking. "What is your business here?" she said, as the man walked towards her, leaving deep foot marks in the volcanic wet sand.

"I'm just here to talk, to make friends," said the man in a deep and guttural tone, which she didn't expect from the look of him.

"I don't talk to strange men on strange beaches in strange places," said she as she put her hand behind her head and looked down towards the ground for a second.

"Ah I'm not a stranger... I am, I think, strange, as a man, but not really a stranger. See, I know you, or am supposed to." Persephone looked up at him quizzically and wondered why this man had business with her. Of all places, times, and lives she's lived, she's never expected to have business with a swarthy-looking man about mid-thirties, especially since, after so many lifetimes of solitude, she's just gotten used to her cage. She rubbed the top of her head boyishly with her left hand and felt uncomfortable having this conversation, having to talk to this nobody.

"I'm not sure that you are supposed to know me. I have been around here for a long time and never seen anyone new. Are you the friend of wind? Do you know the wind?" She finally realized that maybe the legend she'd heard from the fish hag was true.

"Well," said the man, "I am not aware of anyone knowing me per se, but I did meet Jolene, or whatever Jolene is. I have been staying with St. Lazarus and I was told to talk to you and to be your friend." Drops of sweat fell from his forehead as he looked down, picking out a piece of old newspaper that was rolled up into a ribbon from his pocket. He stretched his arm out and grabbed Persephone by the hand and put the paper in it. "Read it," said he as he reached into his pocket and pulled out a tin full of cigarettes and a three-star Swedish match box. He put a cigarette into his pursed lips and tried twice unsuccessfully to light it, finally getting it on the third attempt. "I just picked up smoking," he said as he looked at her face. "I kind of like it."

Persephone opened her hand and unwound the newspaper. It read in bold dark lettering "SEDUCE PERSEPHONE." She immediately felt a strong emotion and pull towards leaving this man's company. "What is this? Seduce me? Where did you get this?" she said, pointing an angry finger at the paper in her palm. The man, who looked visibly uncomfortable for making her feel uncomfortable, began to swallow a little harder than he had before and sighed as he rolled his eyes back, not in an attitude of sarcasm, but in one of pure shame.

"Listen, Persephone. I don't want to do anything weird here with you. I don't feel like it's good for anyone. I don't want to seduce you. I don't want to sleep with you. I don't care. But if you would like to talk and have a conversation, maybe we can find a common thread and become friends, 'cause honestly you seem pretty normal and normal is beyond any expectation."

Persephone wondered about this man as he swayed on the spot where he stood. He offered her an innocent and awkward kindness that she wasn't used to and that made her very uncomfortable. "You make me feel uncomfortable, are you a rat? A bastard?" she said, looking directly into his suntanned face. His look turned from awkwardness to utter shame. She looked him over carefully, trying to figure out his intentions. Persephone had a marvelous eye for people. "You don't seem too cool of a dude," she said as he fumbled his large hand, once again, into his pocket and pulled out a small, cherry-pink, throbbing little mass.

"It's Aphrodite's heart," he said. "It's beating again for the first time in an eternity. Would you like it?" Persephone opened her left hand, and the man slowly placed it into her palm. "I don't think I have a heart," said he as he wiped the sweat off his palms against his very dirty cargo shorts and nervously parted his curly dark hair, licking his chapped lips and then spitting onto the ground as he wobbled like a top that has lost its momentum.

"Are you drunk?" Persephone asked with a pinch of self-importance, for she was a woman who never partook of any alcohol, except on those nights when the fishmonger and St. Lazarus would double team her in the volcanic sand, since sex and power were her only vices.

"Well, I have been drinking more than usual here. Since I have been here, it's kind of like a solid 'wedding drunk,' rum and grog every day, tobacco and magic I guess," said the man as he lit another cigarette and inhaled a deep, wheezy puff that let loose streams of blueish smoke from his nostrils and a waterfall of vapors from his open mouth.

"What's your name?" she asked ruefully. "You know mine somehow, yet I don't know yours. There is an unequal balance of power here, and you have erred in introducing yourself. It's quite rude."

Clipping his thumbs into his belt loops and boyishly swaying forward, the man looked at her with a false bravado and said, "My name is Señor Matanza. I am most likely dead. I am having an adventure, and slowly learning how to tell stories."

Persephone finally smiled after a long period of anxiety. "Uh… Well, are you being honest? You don't seem too terrible a person," she said with a grin she felt silly for showing and wished to hide, still trying to come off as indifferent to the man. To her, now, he seemed harmless, a well-meaning idiot. "Would you like to have a papaya and talk for a bit? Now that we have introduced ourselves, and you seem to have come a long way, I guess it would be okay." Persephone was hoping to evaluate his thoughts and see if he had the capacity to be a friend.

Matanza gurgled out a guttural "Yes" as he blew out the last of his cigarette. She led him to her bamboo cage and pulled out a large brown oilskin bag cinched tight with greased and waterproof rope, opened it, and pulled out what looked like a very large overripe papaya. She bit into it and wiped off the juice with a smile and soft chuckle, offering the fruit to Matanza.

"Here," she said, "it's not too bad." Matanza bit into it and shamelessly slurped up as much as he could. "You have to share, you can't eat all of it," she said, smiling at him. "I don't have much to offer you but a conversation, as you see I live in a cage." Matanza looked up from the papaya and smiled at her.

"It's okay, I'm staying with the holy man St. Lazarus, who has been teaching me how to lie, bullshit, as well as showing me the art of storytelling. Jolene, my other friend, she also helped me learn how to tell stories. I am still struggling to understand St. Lazarus. He is a bygone and worn-out saint." Persephone smiled and looked at him, ever so slightly charmed by his awkwardness, and keeping her knowledge to herself. She knew St. Lazarus quite well—in the carnal sense.

"He's really easy to get off. I know what he likes, and don't worry, most holy men who preach their own good word and are enrobed in enormous power given by their flock, are all glass ego-ed, money-hungry reprobates, who at best hide their crimes and lies. The majority of them embezzle from the stupid and those who are drunk on God," said Persephone. Matanza thought she sounded like a professor.

He looked at her from the depths of the meaty, juicy papaya. "You seem smart, Persephone," he remarked quietly as he threw the rest of the fruit into the volcanic sand and wiped his mouth with his forearm, leaving syrup all over him that stuck the hairs on his arm together. "Can I ask you something, Persephone? How about we just ask each other whatever we want." She again rubbed the back of her head boyishly as she looked down at his dirty feet, still unsure whether to trust him.

"Okay," she said, "but if it becomes too much for me and too honest then you'll have to leave." Persephone controlled her emotions expressing deviancy and expressed her power and sense of self using her body. Honesty and vulnerability were things that she had hidden for many years.

Matanza, confident in his ability to talk and bullshit and tell stories thanks to the help of his friends, looked her over quickly and cleared his throat. "Persephone, do you believe in love? Because I have spent a lot of time thinking about that. I am not whole-hearted enough to believe in love. I don't know if it exists. There seems to be a motivating force throughout our universe that compels people to study, to work, to engage their minds in producing something of value for our collective zeitgeist, a movement of a musical composition perhaps, or a paper on physics and entropy that changes human thought. I have to say that some people are inherent geniuses, some polymaths, others specializing in one thing, while some are as omniscient as Jupiter himself when it comes to their gifts, others are single-minded and selfish. What matters is to waste not what has been endowed to you from whatever one may think created you, and those unique circumstances that educated you into who you are to be. For I have met scholars who are as dumb as bricks in practical matters, and tramps of the road who live like mutts yet survive and thrive on a satchel of apples. Genius has many forms, innumerable as the shells on a seashore, but kindness has one form: selfless love, and that is rarer than any ability acquired or gifted by God." Matanza, equal parts bullshit and truth and seduction, smiled at what he'd just said.

Persephone was intrigued by this man's thoughts and thought back to her life long ago and to those who usurped love, and it made her feel an unendurable sadness. "Matanza," she said as she nervously rubbed her hands along her thighs, wiping off the papaya juice. "I remember my life long ago, and I always think about the love of others. I am quite lonely here. I think I should tell you that if you preach against love or tolerance, and set fire to the passions of the simple-minded masses and move them towards violent discourse, constantly pumping shit and filth into the propaganda machine of whatever state or person that's in power, I would have to tell you that you are on the wrong side of history and that the tales of your corruption and enmity towards those clothed in grace will be cemented for the future to read, and if I could, I would carve those stories into stone myself." She paused for a long second, thinking back to her troubled history. "Matanza, if you are going to become the storyteller and sage here in the outer islands, don't lie to me, and be honest with me, or you will lose a friend."

Matanza looked at her and felt a deep fullness in the pit of his stomach. Maybe it was an attraction to Persephone's brain, which to him seemed wonderful, or maybe it was the overripe papaya. He yet again opened his tin of cigarettes, lit one, and took a deep drag. Matanza ran his fingers through his knotted curly hair, still wet from his swim in the ocean. "Persephone," he said meekly, "what does it feel like when someone loves you? Do you feel anything? Is there an emotion you have or a thought you experience when another person loves you? I don't personally think it exists in a true form; it seems so alien to me. I assume that at some point in my disparate past life I must have loved, but if she or he reciprocated those feelings, how could they be verified? Philosophically one can never know if another is in love with you; there is no test for love-infected blood corpuscles or resonance machines and computerized gadgetry that can tell you the answer. It simply does not compute scientifically. The entire scope of philosophy is to study the blind areas between science and soul, yet no one can prove that love actually exists as anything other than the muttering few gasps for breath one gives after a passionate kiss and some fluttering irregular heartbeats. So if anyone tells you they love you, I would take it in Sartre's definition of bad faith, and also his definition of authenticity, and study it with dense critical theory. For most people lie about love, and it needs as much skepticism as you can afford it." Persephone smiled, feeling a great happiness in this talk with Matanza. She felt a great vulnerability, unsure and afraid about trusting him. She thought that she must overcome her fear. Mantaza interrupted her thoughts. "Oh, and filial piety and friendship, that is part of my whole 'love' bullshit." Persephone smiled.

"Matanza," she said quietly, "are we equals? Do you think you can be my equal and I yours? Can we both respect that in each other?" Matanza gave her a questioning glance and smiled at her, his tanned face showing a blush of embarrassment since he didn't want this answer to be bullshit or improvised as he had been learning.

"Persephone, yes, if not equals, you are more than me, since I think that my past sins have formed me into something hateful." She looked at him with an expression of silent caring and put her arm around his shoulder as friends do. She gambled on putting her arm around him. She was hoping to read him. Surprised by the greasy sweat on his shoulder, Persephone thought to herself, "There are some men who would take my arm on them as an invitation to screw, some as a gesture of friendship, and others just as the way the human animal communicates in its most base 'ape-ness,' our wild form."

"Matanza," she said, walking him away from the cage, past the fish hag's pots and pans, past the nets and towards the beach. "Every man and woman is created in the same vacuum, that strange amniotic galaxy as broad as a starry night, which by sheer unimaginable luck coalesces strange cells into a beating heart, and some people think that even with that axiom, that law, the idea that nobody on this planet is formed any different, shown in the mathematical jurisprudence that governs Euclid: things that are equal to the same thing are also equal to one another. If equals are added to equals, then the wholes are equal; if equals are subtracted from equals, then the remainders are equal, things that coincide with one another are equal to one another. When we finally, one day, far into the future, realize that we have been silly and work together, then we can say to all peoples everywhere, that the whole of ourselves is greater than its parts, and we are all the same. I think that together we can be bigger than ourselves."

Matanza felt a deep yearning to be a good friend to Persephone, to offer her the promise that he would be there for her if she ever needed him, and he was beginning to see that he could trust her as well. "If I were to be a friend to you, Persephone, if I could speak open and honestly, would it lead to pain?" She thought back to the thousands of men throughout her many lives that promised love and friendship and always ran, leaving her in the lurch to suffer. She thought of their fear and how they were just children in dark suits and size 38 jeans and work boots, kids who inhabited a man's frame.

"I cannot promise you anything, Matanza, but don't be weak with me if you choose to be my friend, and I consent to letting you. What bothers me the most is men who vacillate; weak-spined men who hold only the opinion of the masses that support them. You'll see them in churches and politics, in every branch of law and philosophy; rarely does one man stray from the pack. Men are pack animals; you see this in identity politics, liberality versus conservatism. There is no middle, only in the words of whatever each government sets forth in their constitutional papers, the lies they weave, the laws they break; and those people who always stray. History repeats itself, perpetually, always, ad-infinitum. I say the same for women as well, and for scholars, theologians, people in power in general. It's an odd state of being, power, that is. I like to feel powerless; it makes me sexually aroused. I loathe the men who tie me up and use me, St. Lazarus and the fishmonger, but I love the feeling of being used. Yet I am the one who controls their desires, and in some way, I am more powerful than those who use me. As if government were a whore like me, she retains control, and the powers will always exist in her. Of course, all power is female, it's a matriarchal concept, since through her leaders are birthed, and ideas of love and grace are consummated into reality." She paused for a second to gather her thoughts. "If you choose to care for me, or love me, or be my friend, I will have power over you and then we won't be equals anymore."

Matanza walked into the cold sea and dipped his hands in the water, running his fingers again through his hair, then stroked his stubbly beard and pushed back the mustache across his lips. "Love is real, friendship is real, Persephone, even if I don't believe it or feel it; it has to exist. I know deep down in my heart that there is something moving everything, and maybe through telling stories, I can find it."

Persephone interjected right as Matanza finished his thought. "There is a sharp contrast between what is real and what is not," she said in a strong voice. "Most of it stems from the confusion between facts and opinions. I have been thinking about this for a very long time, since I have been here before you, and alone. There is truth, and there is goodness and virtue. To be virtuous you must live and act as what you wish to become. This we all face at some point. Some people realize it when they have been fucked over, screwed, used and discarded; some fortunate ones read about virtue and justice before they get torn to pieces, rarely does that happen. Now do you think that to be virtuous and just, that you must take from another who wrongs you? Is reciprocity justice? If one man steals my clothing, as just punishment should someone steal his? I think that if a system of value existed besides money, then justice would be fairer. For we assign the value of things to money and the taking and dividing of it with reciprocal justice. But what if you fall in love with me, or we become trusted friends, and I take your heart and ruin it, if I steal your words and use them, or speak ill of you? Would you taking mine, or having me pay, bring you justice? No, in love there is no justice, in its rawness it hurts the most, and people still dream of finding someone who can hurt them, piece by piece. Some even forgive each other for the terrible things they do. To be just, one should love the law. To be virtuous, one must love and understand oneself, albeit humbly; but there is no justice in romantic love, only in filial piety and friendship." She paused again and gathered her thoughts as best she could. "Señor Matanza, you must have been gifted Aphrodite's heart for a reason, for even if you were the Tigermother, and a terrible man, you must be able to be trusted with hearts, and I in turn will trust you with mine." Matanza sat looking at her, incredibly grateful for a real conversation. He took her arm from around his shoulder and gently held her hand and they swayed with the ocean breeze like two little children. He looked at her and smiled.

"Persephone, I was told it was all relative, that love and suffering is all relative. In fact, I think I believe that. What may be suffering to me may not be to you, and what you may think is love is nothing but a burning under your belly fat that leads you into a bad decision. I don't think that two people can love each other, and to think that there is only one person on Earth for you is mythologizing the fractured obsession that happens between all people, everyone is broken. There are many people at many different seasons of our lives... you happen to be here now, but if it were any other place at some other time; I would be forced to make another friend, a different friend." Matanza looked down in confusion. "I wouldn't think too highly of the 'there is one love of your life' idea, either. I wouldn't know the benefits of only one person. We are all born with one appendix, and it can kill you—sometimes you need to remove it to save yourself. All of life, all of love, hatred, relationships, friendships, they take incredible amounts of work; people don't realize how much work it takes to love someone truly and they give up when the fairytale feelings subside, which they do, for everyone, all the time. Love is absolute, like the thought and concept of a creator, a truth that one need not experience with another to know is true."

Persephone smiled for a second because she realized she was having an honest grown-up conversation that mattered, that Matanza would be the best storyteller on the islands, and that she liked his concepts of personal freedom, work, and love. She thought he was splendid for having just met him, and he thought the same of her. "Do you know me, Matanza? Do you know my story, my history?"

He looked confused, he knew absolutely nothing except how to bullshit and tell tales. "I don't," said he with a hint of sadness in his voice. "I would love to learn about you and what makes you who you are and take my time to listen and be there for you if you wish," he said as honestly as he could.

Persephone smiled a large and white toothy smile and rubbed his head as one pets a well-behaved dog. "I know your story," she said as he looked up in surprise. "I know everything you have done and will do, and everything that brought you here. You were the Tigermother, and a man of consequence who broke his connection with any divinity of your own volition. But like you said, 'Suffering is relative.' You met the her/him Babirusa in your dreams, the whole duality, they are your friend, right? Or were until they couldn't save you. Well, let me tell you a little of my past," she said as she sat him down crossed legged and kept his hand in hers. "When I was a human, thousands of years ago, there was an old magic in the deep words from the priestesses and oracles of the gods. There were kings and queens and warriors; there was a female genius and a male genius; there was a beautiful duality in human nature that governed us in balance; there was a strong matriarchy, even in the gnostic gospels of the Christians that were hidden away by those who controlled language; they understood the grand design of the genderless female/male, the androgyny that gave birth to us all and our ideas and religions. Slowly, the magic corroded and was worn away like sandstone through years of rain, and the equal geniuses of both men and women were thrown out of balance pendulously to one extreme or the other, and we are now struggling to find the middle." She looked at him with a graceful expression. "Let's try to find our middle here together, all we have is time," she said, almost purring it out like a sleepy female lioness.

Señor Matanza was finding it very easy to connect with Persephone, and he enjoyed the way she expressed her thoughts openly and honestly. He looked up at her as they were sitting on the beach, hand in hand, filled with childlike wonder at each other's thoughts. "I will be the best storyteller I can. I think that with you around, and if we are honest with each other, we can make great tales of wonderful magic and happiness."

Persephone smiled at him; he had surpassed any expectation she could have looked for in a friend. She looked him over carefully, his thick shape, and his belly and chest seemed as if it could bring safety to her. "You have to be a leader here," she said as she struggled to keep from smiling at him forever. "There is an invisible fabric of areligious morality that holds all people in all nations and places together; how dangerous it is when leaders are not a people's moral compass and do not attempt to weave in length and breadth to the fabric; how dangerous it is when they weave in strands from some ideology and not just open-hearted and honest goodness. You have to be our compass."

Matanza felt as though he could accomplish anything with Persephone as his friend and wondered why he had to learn how to tell stories, to lie and bullshit, to seduce with language, when it just took him being honest to develop his affection and respect for her. Maybe they were only exercises in building confidence. He grabbed her other hand. "Is this okay? Me holding your hand? Does it make you uncomfortable?" he asked, finally realizing that he was moved to hold her without thinking.

"It's okay," she said kindly, "but thank you for asking." She wondered if ever a man would have the confidence to understand that sometimes, within boundaries, it is ok to take a hand. She mindlessly drifted into a quote: "When there is understanding then we can steal little pieces of others, but we must build trust." It went unheard.

"Tell me a little about myself, just for a second, Persephone. We have much time here and many things to talk about. I just want to hear something from my life." Matanza grew a little nervous, unsure if he was ready to hear her story, or a piece of it. However, he realized that in this moment was the only feeling of safety he'd had here.

"I'll say this to you, and with time you can hear *your* story," said Persephone with a small amount of trepidation. "The last line you hear before a group of people dies, as it gurgles its last breath, bloodied from its slit throat, is only a whisper of what could have been if the social order were in the hands of the people themselves and not balled up in the pockets of the rich and the powerful. It's happened, you've seen it happen, you fought for it to happen, in some way, your own strange way, and you hoped to stop it. You were an arsonist, always fanning the flames and adding crude oil to the wads of paper money, cash that fueled your people's conflicts and interests. You were an absolute animal and the Tigermother. I hope you've changed. I will have to study you, for the proper study of an honest man is man himself, and I don't want to care for a man who is still burning with cruelty."

Matanza was sad to learn he was a cruel and complicated man and hoped that he could be forgiven, and he wished he could hear his story so he could feel all the pain he'd once caused and suffer the heart-wrenching remorse that he thought he deserved. He looked away from Persephone for a second and gathered his emotions. "You say you enjoy being used, that it gives you power, and that you think it healthy. Well, I feel nothing for any beating heart in a bottle, and nothing for any illusionary goddess at the bottom of the sea, nothing for a mad holy man, a defrocked saint of dubious consequence. In fact, the more I realize the less I care, and the more at peace I feel. Maybe eons ago, or just yesterday, or whenever it was I was knee deep in blood and conflict, I cared too much, or thought too much; but I think I may have been broken back then, a shoddy oriental gimmicky bauble that breaks the moment one puts batteries in it. I feel nothing for your pain and suffering, nor do I care how you treat yourself or your unabashed sexual deviance. It makes me happy to talk inconsequentially about what makes you happy, what makes me happy, and somehow about something where we can both grow together, and maybe I can find forgiveness for my past."

Persephone smiled a wide smile again; she knew she could redeem this idiosyncratic wobbly man, perpetually grogged and chain-smoking strange cigarettes. "If you could tell me a story through a character's ideas and thoughts instead of the narrative, that would be quite something. I'll tell you your story as I know your thoughts better than who you were," said Persephone smiling. Matanza moved in and hugged her like a grizzly bear, a bit unwelcome and surprising, forced, and off.

Persephone feigned comfort and grit a smile through anxiety and vulnerability.

"I hope I didn't just meet another man I will be forced to loathe," she thought to herself. "I don't want to be paranoid."

Matanza couldn't help laughing at her. "You're into some weird shit, right? Well, I wouldn't know much about kink or perversity, but maybe in the future, you know, would you consider getting weird? We are kind of stuck here alone."

"No, I'd rather just talk and eat papayas with you until I pass out," she said as Matanza showed the dead-eyed face of a man who went in awkwardly and was shutdown with a punch to the gut.

She chuckled for a moment and got very serious but still had a large toothy grin on her face. "I'm not going to stop fucking the fishmonger, and St. Lazarus. I like to get spit roasted on occasion by them both, tied up and slapped, choked and gagged, but if you think you can handle my occasional traipses with the other men on these islands, then you can be my best friend, and we can talk, write books, and read them to each other before we fall asleep from overripe papayas."

Matanza felt a healthy dose of jealousy, but he knew she only wanted pure freedom. "What I have realized, Persephone, is that I am a man who is in control of all of his appetites. I don't need what other men need, or what they think they do, be it the sour taste of a woman's wetness, or any pleasures that men desire, and if you tell me my story, of what I was, of who I was, then I will approach you in as much kindness, compassion, and love as I have tamed myself not to feel. For if a man is to rise above all others, he must be his own tyrant and assuage all his wants with only the barest of necessities, so when the moment comes for him to take a partner and share with her a communion of two bodies as one, then he will appreciate her with all that's left of his heart."

She looked up at him from his big brawny bear hug. "That's a pretty good answer for a dude that just got ruthlessly shut down." She said, while secretly thinking that he was the type of man either to ignore all subtlety and nuance, not care whatsoever; or a reformed bad-boy that got so screwed up that he is now as dense as a sack of wrenches.

Matanza smiled. "Have I seduced you then?"

Persephone laughed. "No, you haven't, let's just look at the sea and eat as many rotten papayas as possible."

St. Vitus the Fishmonger

8

The smell of dirty skin and sweat was thick in the air. I didn't realize that a woman could sweat so much from a night of papaya feasting and sleeping. I sat with her head on my thigh as she slept, my hands holding my body up as I leaned back. I thought of what my past adventures could have been and wondered at my mysteries. I vacillated on whether she could only be a friend in my future, or maybe a lover? Or hoping against hope, maybe even my partner? My confusion on the matter was a dilemma. Would a strong-willed and intelligent woman want me? I would have to be resolute and choose, and maybe persuade her not to see the other men on these strange islands. However, I also thought that she only wanted freedom. In some way she was the freest of us all. I remembered reading Dante long ago and thought back words: "The darkest places in hell are reserved for those who maintain their neutrality in times of moral crisis."[26]

---

[26] . This quote was playing, looped, on a cassette recorder when the author awoke from falling asleep at the typewriter after ingesting incredible quantities of benzodiazepines and alcohol. For months, the author of this book thought he had composed the quote originally. It was finally made clear upon editing by a reader, that it was Dante.

Persephone moaned a sleepy, satisfying yawn and mumbled in her sleep, "Can you pick me up and carry me to my cage?" I slowly rose and picked her up. She was much heavier than I anticipated, and I barely managed to carry her three feet before having to take a break. She mumbled some dream nonsense and put her arms around my neck. I thought aloud, "God, this woman is heavier than she seems. So much for a strong man being able to handle this." She smiled and rested her head on my chest. I panted and made it another few yards. "Dammit, what does this woman eat? Christ," I said under my breath as I struggled to open the lid of her cage and gently put her in. She rolled over on her belly as I shut the lid and locked her in. The straw bedding reeked of piss. I tapped the top of the box and walked down towards the ocean. The ocean was blue and bright, the sun reflecting off of the tips of the waves and the water seeming as if it weren't moving far off in the distance. I stared at it as the waves cracked onto the shore and the white sand felt like flour under my feet, seabirds laughed as they rode the air above me, and the dune grasses swayed happily in the wind. The sun was a large yellow crescent that illuminated the beach, the black rocks, and the white sand. The clouds, grey and brown against the sky, looked like gigantic, drooping mammary glands that shone silvery at their round bottoms. A large albatross flapped by my head and sent a whooshing poof of air all around me that lifted me off my feet. I grabbed for its tail feathers as it flew by and rode the wind into the cloudy heights.

I stood for a moment that seemed eternal and noticed a thickness to the air, a sweetness and milkiness. There was a smell in the air. I couldn't put my finger on it; it smelled of flowers, not the sweet smell of flowers from the altar of a wedding ceremony, but the saccharine and thick smell of floral wreaths at a funeral. It permeated everything. I could imagine it smelled like the chapel of the Egyptian doctors and priests that burned incense while mummifying the pharaohs deep in the bowels of the funeral chambers while slaves battered the air with palm-frond fans. Suddenly I heard a shrill laugh and a nasal voice from nowhere. "I think you ought to p-pursue p-p-pleasure above all else, within your moral boundaries, that is. It is a method of ethical relativism," the voice said.

There at the mouth of a craggy footpath, where black porous volcanic boulders made an arch, and a lifetime's accumulation of seagull shit was caked on its top like the white and green drippings of an enormous tallow candle, stood a man, bent over from age, his head bald and suntanned except for the white locks of hair that rounded and bordered his skull. He was shiny, and his brown skin glistened in the sun; his nose large and hooked like the beak on a strange bird of prey. His arms, which were taut and muscled, still somehow seemed thin and long like boiled noodles. His bare feet were too large for his frame, and his calves shone hairless as if they had been oiled. He held a liter of Turbo King beer[27] in his left hand that was sweating in the sun. His right arm lay bent over his shoulder as he was carrying enormous ocean beasts that were tied together with a blue polyester rope through their gills. After popping open the top of the cold bottle with his scarred

---

[27] . "Turbo King" being a lager of Rwandan manufacture, with notes of dry wheat and bran. It is top heavy when poured cold into a glass, and best consumed on nights when the rain is heavy, and the thunder loud.

and worn hand, he took a swig of the brew and finished it with a loud and crisp "AHHHH," followed by a "That's what I'm talking about" in between satisfied exaltations.

"Ethical relativism?" I said aloud to my companion. "Pleasure?"

He began walking over to me, jerking his body strangely. Finally, there stood before me an old man with gnarled and arthritic fingers, grizzled hair around his shiny bald head, knobby knees, and a bowed back. He grimaced, contorted his face, and shuddered and shook with clumsiness and uncontrollable, bizarre, non-repetitive movements of the body and face. He was an acute sufferer of Huntington's chorea. He looked up at me since he was short and small and, while he winced away with dyskinesia, muttered some nonsensical words under his breath and stared at my face. His shoulders rocked and rolled in their joints. "You must be Señor Matanza," he said as he took a swig from the bottle of cold beer that seemed always full. He smacked and puckered his lips as his mouth contorted arrhythmically.

"Yes, I am," I said as I looked at the bottle and licked my lips expectantly. "But you have the advantage over me, sir, for I do not know who you are," said I.

He smiled, showing a false grin of stained, irregular teeth. "My name is St. Vitus the Fishmonger," he said as he took another swig of the Turbo King, followed by a loud and crisp "Ahhh."

"You're on the beach vacillating on what to do with Persephone, right? Well, that pussy is as sweet as peach pie and tart like a Florida lime, isn't it? But is it worth it?" He took another swig and wiped his puckered lips with the back of his hand.

"I would not know what is or is not peachy or limey. I did not have to opportunity to taste her," I said as I looked him over and wondered why of all people would Persephone choose to let herself get railed by this absurd anomaly.

St. Vitus looked at me. "Let me tell you something, Señor Matanza, or is it the 'Tigermother'?" He continued after a short pause. "There is really no magic, only the deep magic between two people's bodies. That pulse you feel that draws your loins to another's, that longing in the pit of your stomach that feels empty when your lover isn't there, that sourness of your lover's moistness on your mouth that gets shared when one explores another's body, tasting everything, loving everything, and losing nothing, nothing but your complete self into someone else. That's the magic that you are looking for, right? Persephone has that magic and it keeps this place alive."

I looked at St. Vitus quizzically, lit a cigarette, and blew the smoke over his head. "She's that important to the ecosystem of this place?" I asked.

He looked up at me, squinted, and grabbed my face with his hands, feeling it as a blind person would when they meet someone. "There is a place where the strong medicine and the deep magic commingle. It is far from the knowledge of men, and only three of the gods ever knew of it. From this place come those beasts of anxiety, lust, and disinhibition that overwhelm us when we drown in other people's bodies and inhale the smoke and perfume of deviant fornication in all its glory. It is a wonderful feeling when one breaks all the religious sex laws and, without piety, worships another person's body, smell, and taste. Dive in headfirst if you ever find yourself with Persephone. Take whatever chance you may get. Find religion and morality upon her lips. She is our salvation."

"Is she a witch or a deity? A duende or a jinn? What matter is she composed of? For us to find a home in her, then she must be of graceful origins," I asked St. Vitus as I inhaled a long and crackling drag of my cigarette, the cherry growing long and red, blue smoke rising off the end and trailing away like a floating cobweb.

St. Vitus blew across the top of the bottle and it made a sonorous sound that resembled the warning horn of a train. He smiled happily, showing his chipped and cracked teeth. "What is Persephone made of, you ask?" he said as he laughed and took a heavy sip from the ever-full glass liter of beer. "What do you think about 'The Absolute,' Señor Matanza? That which is unconditioned and uncaused by anything else, that which is a perfect and self-caused eternal being, the essence of everything that existed and will exist, which cannot be conceived of."

I took the last drag off my smoke and crumpled the remainder between my index finger and thumb. The ocean breeze bellowed as if it were filling the sails on a tall ship, the wind whipping the locks of my curly hair. "St. Vitus, I have never considered that kind of concept or thought much on anything other than my histories and what is presented before me, that which I devour or save for later, drink up or not drink. I find that here I only live statically and purely in the moment."

St. Vitus jerked all over his body like a baby giraffe taking its first steps, as if he were dancing to a strange and scratched record. He laughed again and spat on the ground through his gapped front teeth. "What if I were to tell you that Persephone is our answer to a cosmological argument? That all of this, this eternity, this absurdity, and all of its parts can neither be accidental nor self-caused." He looked at me seriously, smiled, and continued. "Maybe you caused them, Señor Matanza, maybe you somehow have echoed like a scream over mountain tops and valleys and created this, or maybe it is Persephone, maybe what is real is only firelight shadows and pictures on cave walls, or maybe it is what you will write here in between the pages of a book."

I looked at St. Vitus as he teetered and jiggled away. The wattle of loose skin on his neck swayed around like a hefty scrotum on a warm day. "What about the carpenter who preached?" I said as I stood mesmerized by the man's old chicken neck. "I heard that he is the god of influence these so many eons, is that not an absolute?"

St. Vitus took a still greater chug of the ice-cold Turbo King beer, the liquid disappearing from the bottle, and then refilling itself after his long and winding satisfied exhalation—like those cheap toy baby doll milk bottles that magically empty and refill themselves when you shove them into a doll's plastic face.

St. Vitus looked up at me. "What do I think about Jesus, my man?" He picked at his teeth and started singing a sea chantey about stout ales and cold Belgian lambics, then he stopped momentarily and stared off into the cloudy sky. "Oh boy oh boy, Jesus, you ask? Yes... He was a rioter and troublemaker. Now he had some good ideas and all, but like all good ideas they tend to last longer than their expiration date. He should have gotten himself a pretty girl, drank a lot of wine, and eaten ergot-infested rye bread, seen what life would be like while hallucinating, and he would have been much less wound up." St. Vitus put his liter of Turbo King down and pointed his gnarled and arthritic index finger at my nose. "Some say Christ is the prototype, the proto-man." He stopped for a second, licked his chapped lips, and continued. "I heard this once from a young, skinny, knobby-kneed, curly-haired teenage nun who would give the priests hand jobs when they were stressed and suck them off after confession and while they knelt at the pews on rainy autumn evenings. She hated herself and her choices, yet she would gasp whenever I said that Christ's existence was absurd and that it's important to revel in the comedy of it. If we are to say that he is the protohuman or the first step in development of the Western man, the thinking Western man, then we are giving him undue credit. If you have any doubt that he was anything but a facile-minded man who preached social equity and kindness—maybe the foremost philosopher of kindness, but not the protohuman or first thinking Western man—then you are imbecilic. What of the thousands of other gods that have populated our shared historical fiction? Why are we not celebrating the atomists, or the Platonic thinkers, or Epicureans? Why has God chosen to live two thousand years ago as man and not presently? I think that the modern man and woman should worship themselves and their impressive minds—when developed well—hopefully altruistically and gracefully as providers for families and lovers of humanity. The developed human being should be as kind as Christ, yet unyielding and as strong as the boughs of a willow, bending in the wind yet never breaking. They should be self-sufficient and impervious to words that cut, and their tongues should be as broad as a lion's and as sharp as a dagger, and their backs and chests as broad as a dragon's, their arms as soft as a bear's to hold their loved ones close, and their fingers mustard-yellow talons as sharp and curved as an eagle's, and their bellies as soft as a seal's or an otter's so when they are supine their children can rest on them and sleep content and warm as if wrapped in summer clouds and pressed on by a steady and kind hand."

I stood awed at St. Vitus' words and wondered at the argument of his prose. "St. Vitus," I said as I slowly dipped down to pick up the liter of beer because I wanted so much to taste it, "how did you hear that from the novitiate nun?" I finally put my hand around the bottle, at which St. Vitus smiled and shook his head disapprovingly.

"I was a priest years ago, lifetimes ago, and I preached liberation theology in the steamy Guyanan jungles. We met in the understory of the verdant bush of the equatorial forest. She loved me, and I her. We would talk and tell each other tales. In innocence we became lovers and together hid our youngling from the church, conceived in graceful caring, a moppet that came from awkward love and godless self-loathing. She was disappeared by the oppressive laity who ran the right-wing death squads, as was the child, and I swore to worship another less jealous God."

A strong feeling of pity wore and bit at my bones; so pitiful a physical specimen and so sad a tale bothered me. St. Vitus cleared his throat as thinking of his nun brought him a deep emotion. "Where should I look for wisdom and scholarship?" I asked St. Vitus quizzically.

"Are you not to be the scribe and storyteller here?" he exclaimed in surprise as if I did not know. "You should find wisdom in yourself and your mind. I would forget finding wisdom in any church. I wouldn't think too highly of the scholars and teachers of the church. The church doctors were mainly a group of sinners and apostates that maligned most of Western moral thinking behind closed doors and reveled in a false and bastard catechism. Years ago, they all shared a goatskin of sweet wine and a lunch of dates, olives, and figs as they sought to rewrite the gospels under the heady influence of too much incense and Eastern perfumes. Ambrose, Augustine, Gregory the Great, and Jerome all wore habits made from the skins and feathers of the last living phoenix, which was finally caught by one of Davinci's wooden machines, and Gregory kept a diamond-encrusted vial of tears taken from pox-infected crippled orphans in the crook of his gold crozier."

I grabbed at the cold beer again, but this time St. Vitus took it from me and said, "No no no. It is my shame to suffer an unquenchable thirst, an altschmerz and desire to pound back cold beer. I must say that if you drink from this bottle then you too will have to drink the brew for all time, tying you to this place for eternity."

"How am I to learn and tell stories if I am not to drink in this place in its totality and not read the wisdom of the gospels and the legends of this place?" I said, feeling a little miffed that I couldn't drink the refreshing beer. "I think you are better off getting a library card and using it, instead of letting some sad-sack professor like St. Lazarus influence you. All that matters in life is the ability to read and write, as Jolene Armitage told me eons ago—and you, recently. Studying, notating, re-reading, talking, and telling stories is all that really matters; everything revolves around reading and using linguistics: the power of analyzing language. Just talk to us, Señor Matanza, and listen with what's left of your heart, and tell us stories," said St. Vitus with a trembling lip.

I looked closely at him and thought it kind that Persephone chose to love him in her own way. I am nobody to judge her, and she deserves all freedoms if her duty here is to be our salvation. If she is to engage us all in love, then I am nobody but a poor man to think ill of her. I thought that I should grow up and understand that there are multiple types of love, as broad as the starry sky, and her saving us from our past sins is the ultimate form of selfless compassion.

"What would you like to do here, Tigermother?" asked St. Vitus as his face palpitated like a broken heart amid an anxiety attack.

"I would like to write a tome one day filled with obscure pieces of great wisdom that nobody will see given the context of the whole work. Only when it is dissected would its grace be noticed in its entire completeness. I hope, if I write it, that it gets thrown into the dustbins of history as a work of nonsensical smoke billowing from yellowing paper pages."

St. Vitus laughed and bared his strange teeth that resembled a fanged baboon's. "You are not pursuing fame or glory? Completing the work in obscurity is enough for you? That is commendable. I ask only that you do your best work and do it with honesty and grace," he said with a wistful look in his eyes.

I saw the emotion in St. Vitus' throbbing and pulsating face. "St. Vitus, how did you come to find this place?" He took another swig from the beer bottle and this time drank it all down, only for the bottle to refill itself once more.

"After a period of great darkness and space, there was a bright light. During my time as a priest in the jungle, I heard tell tales of the big fishes in the deepest parts of the oceans. I heard that some of the beasts looked like women from afar, and swam with webbed fingers and toes, and had beaks as sharp as a falcon's and arms as strong and muscular as a gorilla's, with gilded fur like the Golden Fleece and breasts that would upend and overflow from their tight braziers, and their dairies would fall over like flesh pouring onto glass, their nipples, pink and soft, would become hard and lactate rum for the lost sailors and dying men on wrecked ships to suckle before they perish. I followed the stars in the ocean to this place and have been here since the dawn of time."

"What happened during the darkness before the light?" I asked him; my memory of how I got here was not intact.

He smiled again, put down his bottle, and placed his hands on his hips, rocking back and forth. "I was able to see the universe in its totality for the briefest of moments before I found myself surrounded by a bright light."

My interest was piqued. I almost erupted with joy. I hadn't thought of any place besides these islands. "Tell me, St. Vitus, what is the universe like? Is it beautiful and wholesome and warm?" I asked excitedly.

He leaned over and bade me lower my head so he could whisper in my ear. "Let me delineate to you the composition of the starry night and the system of planets. Under the Earth there lies a great beast, a turtle, and upon his back is the Earth and her sister planets held up by an elephant so large that

50,000 years are needed to walk its circumference, which is the home to us here on the outer islands. Upon the Earth lie the heavens and the sky and stars, and above the sky is a great snake, the devourer of worlds, who has no name; however, his mouth is night, and he swallows galaxies. Above the snake, there is the ten-horned beast of revelations that sits in judgment of our world, and he is held, chained by the muzzle, by the ancient and powerful giantess that we call the 'Whore of Babylon.' She is dressed in crimson robes, a chain and collar wrapped around her neck, and from her breasts and mouth spill the oceans and rivers. We were all birthed from her and will return to her womb, the night sky, to be devoured by the snake and judged by the beast every day and every night for eternity."[28]

I stood in awe of St. Vitus' experience and was consumed with curiosity, as I did not remember anything of my past or where I came from. "What did the universe sound like? What did it smell like?" I asked.

St. Vitus looked contented to talk about this, even while standing shivering from tremors like a cold parrot getting its footing on a cage bar. "As for smell, I don't remember at all, Señor Matanza, but I do remember a guitar playing through the ether, a mellifluous, beautiful tune. I heard one solo guitar string, plucked and thumping over and over, rumbling, like a man who weighs three thousand pounds dancing on a wooden floor in an old Unitarian chapel that holds up all of the sky, galaxies, and the hearth and womb of the world, burning in its fires, bright, over the far-away mountains and skies, as it all

---

[28] . This dialog by St. Vitus is based very loosely on an Islamic creation myth, Norse creation mythos, as well as smatterings form the Book of Revelation.

falls onto the outstretched arms of a beautiful blond-haired and blue-eyed woman who holds in her heart the love of all men and women. It was a lovely thing."

Again, I saw emotion well up in his eyes, and again it brought me feelings of pity. I looked down at St. Vitus' worn old face and confessed to him my jealousies. "I wanted to fight you, St. Vitus, everything about Persephone and me being so confused and lost as to the stories I have to tell here. I don't know if I should stay or leave, punch you or hug you, tell stories as a static character in this odd play, or swim out to the deep ocean never to return and make new adventures for myself."

St. Vitus trembled, and his face contorted into a weird and grotesque smile. "Ah, to fight me, and to fight St. Lazarus, that would require an enormity of virtue and gamesmanship." He paused for a moment and continued. "There is a space where the most consummate of professional duelists falters. It is that moment where their vision exceeds their minds. When you are battling a human in those most peculiar circumstances where wits are needed, you must be one with all the knowledge you have taken into your brain; you must know it and have faith in it, and when you see your adversary overreach or swat at something out of step or just millimeters from their grasp, you must strike and undercut them ruthlessly. All good battles worth your steel will come down to this fact." He stopped and looked at me again with a large, open-eyed expression. "It seems as though you are the type of man who bounces from the extremes of vacillation on one end and confusion on the other, punctuated by moments of incredible, caffeine-induced anxiety, tachycardia, and nervous heart palpitations brought on by too much demon rum. You have a drunken wobble about you," he said as he laughed through his teeth. "You should be more resolute and confident."

I heeded his advice and decided then and there to be a more effective man. "You know your story; do you happen to know mine? I struggle to remember my past. From The Babirusa I learned that I was a terrible and foul beast of a man, Persephone and St. Lazarus echoed that, and I cannot place any memories of what I may have been. I hope that I have grown since then. I don't think that I was ever envious. Envy is the worst of all bad character traits. Most every idea and action based on it is unctuous and slippery. Men and women who covet the circumstances of others are as low to the ground as a serpent. I feel wrong feeling passionate jealousy for a woman of beauty, freedom, and grace such as Persephone. I know I wasn't. I hate it too much and I am capable of more empathetic love than anything. 'Yet, taught by time, my heart has learned to glow for other's good, and melt at other's woe.'"[29]

St. Vitus looked towards the ground in sadness before he responded. "You were a terrible human being, Matanza—as we all were—you were a beast, and one who lived for the happiness of causing suffering. The only forgiveness and redemption you will find is in Persephone's sweetest parts. Embrace the fact that she is mother to us all and nurtures us who have never loved in our lives, who hated and feared others, and lived to hurt. In some ways she splays herself out open-armed as we all ravish her, and in her nature and her

---

[29]. An oratory by Homer, crystallized and written down by others throughout history.

biology and self, she takes our sins—as we bury our pain—deep into the yonic parts of her soul and forgives us. We are the forgotten as she is our redeemer. Remember that."

I didn't want to hear anything else about me. I was responsible for horrors and deep down I knew it. "St. Vitus," I said before I paused for a moment to formulate a question. "Will death redeem me?"

St. Vitus' smile went away, and he looked lost in thought and emotion for a moment. "Tigermother… the day you die I will shepherd you on your way. I can imagine that the day you are to be judged by whatever holy or unholy thing presides at the end of your life, that when I introduce you to the pantheon of the gods as a traveler in that new realm, I will be heard announcing to the angels in heaven, and those many that have fallen, the words of Cicero: 'I have brought before you, judges, not a thief, but a plunderer; not an adulterer, but a ravisher; not a mere committer of sacrilege, but the enemy of all religious observance and holy things[30].'"

St. Vitus grabbed my arm and dragged me away from the beach and took me to Persephone's cage where she lay sleeping. He dug his hand into the pocket of his shorts and pulled out a wadded and crinkly paper ball, put it in my hand, closing my fist over it, and held my hand. "Now, as she sleeps, tell her that you are learning to feel remorse, tell her you were wicked; pray to her for forgiveness."

Emotion rode over his face like the dark clouds and wind that were whipping around us. I stood motionless for a

---

[30] . The Instituto Oratoria of Quintillian. Books VII-IX. As noted in Cicero's denouncing of Verres.
(Amplification or Attenuation)

moment. His dry and gnarled palm covering my closed fist with the paper inside, he rested his head on my shoulder. "Go ahead, Tigermother, tell her."

The words flowed naturally as I opened my mouth, athough my redeemer was asleep, and she didn't hear them. Deep down I hoped the prayer would be heard. A strong emotion gripped me, and I choked back gasps. "There is a happiness that comes from faith and worship, a satisfaction and feeling of wholesome filial love that is satiating and warm. I choose to worship the smell of flowers after you bathe, and the saltiness of your tears and your friendship. In some way your filial connection with me will be my communion wafer, and with every idea we share, concern we speak of, and song we write together, I will be more and more capable of being your friend, and in you, I find the universal truth of loving myself as well, and all of God's creatures, marvelous in their diversity as the freckles upon your soft skin. Forgive me."

St. Vitus smiled at me and told me to open my hand. Inside, I found a wadded-up piece of bubblegum wrapper with twine and yarn strung from it. I opened it slowly, and I found the words "Seduce Persephone" scrawled on the inside in primary school crayon. St. Vitus looked at me and said, "I was just like you once, when I first got here, and I have dedicated my life to being saved. The choice is up to you whether to stay or leave, love or be forgiven." St Vitus lit a small fire on the ground near Persephone's cage; poured onto it myrrh, incense, and oils from a bottle in his pocket; smoke rose over and around us, dipped in between our three bodies, and carried with it the grotesque and thick aroma of each of us. It filled my nostrils and burned my lungs when I inhaled it, like a ghost or specter from my past. St. Vitus looked at me and held my upper arm tightly. "Mankind is poised midway between the gods and the beasts,"[31] he said as he let go of my arm, walked back through the arched black stone outcropping, and disappeared back into the fuming smoke that surrounded us.

---

[31] . As written by Plotinus.

The story, the self, and the spirit

9

I walked far from the mouth of the craggy rocks that St. Vitus had disappeared into, far from Persephone. I walked long and far across the beach where the mid-morning sun hung so low across the branches of the palm tree that it looked as though it would stay there, perched happily with the seagulls and albatrosses. The wind picked up, and very soon the sun began to get lower and lower on the horizon. The wind shuddered the palm trees and the rustle of fronds drowned out the occasional creak and groan of the trunks in heavy gusts; a sand crab pitter pattered over my feet; my toes sank deep in the pliant, pastel grit; and I heard the gawk of a seabird and the rush of waves on the shore as I cater-cornered over the sand for what seemed like eons, the sun now lying low and loose, as meek as a ground-level peach. I was wracked with hunger pangs, for I had not eaten in what seemed like a few weeks (time is fluid here on the outer islands). I reached into my pocket to see if I had a piece of chewing gum or a candied orange peel or any cinnamon I could chew, maybe bits of Persephone's left-over papaya or a fishbone I could suckle on. I reached in and searched with my fingers and was only able to pull out the small paper packet that St. Vitus had given me, his invitation to seduce Persephone. I opened it, untying its strings, and as I looked at it again, slowly the letters began to change, to bleed back into the paper like watered-down ink, and reformed themselves into another phrase in beautiful copperplate calligraphy: "Dear Señor Matanza, roll me up and smoke me."

I was taken aback by the invitation to smoke an alien collection of papers and twine, but again I thought of the magic of this place and chose to roll up a fat and lumpy cigar from it dexterously with my thick fingers. I pulled out the yellow box of Swedish three-star matches and lit it on the third try, just as the wind was blowing my fire out. I took a few puffs to get the cherry going and finally sucked in drag after drag.

Slowly I began to feel an unendurable panic and anxiety that shot through my body and shuddered each singular nerve in unison. My eyes shut tight in a knee-jerk reflex. I was becoming acutely aware of being surrounded by everything and all matter that was vaguely horrible, dirty, mean, and of a fear of suffering great violence. I tried to mutter out a cry for help but only heard a choking and gargling sound that I somehow voiced as my tongue had gone deep against my throat. Everything that was and had been or ever would be obscurely abominable and hideous was all around me. An uncontrollable fear led me to grunt out sobs. I fell to the sand, blind with emotional agony and indescribable dread that lasted for what seemed like decades.

"Hey! Heyo!" I heard softly in my own voice, but I knew I wasn't saying anything. "Hey, Matanza! Wake up!" I slowly started to rise to my knees as if I were fighting a great weight or pressure on my shoulders. It seemed an Atlantean task to even get to my knees, but slowly, and ever cautiously, I was able to reach a hunched over stance, like a cripple with terrible and maltreated spina bifida, a crippled centaur speared through his horse haunches. I opened my eyes and looked up. The sun was distended and engorged, purple and blue like bruises on a beaten man's face, the gloaming twilight redolent with the breath of the ocean, and flying fish the size of shiny new Cadillacs, with tails like a red-breasted robin's and with paws of an otter, dibbled and nodded through the tops of the waves, soaring for brief moments like so many ideas and dreams, happy memories and nightmares of past peoples. The sparrows and bats seemed like dangerous, enormous, man-eating, fanged, flying beasts as they dipped towards the left then rose slowly into the evening sky, listing to and fro as they jolted and lurched upwards apprehensively into the grey barren west. Everything around me had the feeling of a dark and violet and green-tinged nightmare.

I was able to focus my eyes straight ahead. Standing before me I saw a ghostly outline of a thick-set man emerge in olive drab military clothing, his shirt unbuttoned halfway, showing a sweat-glistened and hairy chest where an upside-down crucifix hung from a bronze chain. He had a tiger-stripe camouflage boonie cap pushed back upon his head, brown curls around its fringe, sun-chapped lips, and deep brown skin. He had worn black leather boots, his trousers bloused inside of them, and he stood arms crossed, proud, but with a look of being dangerous deep set upon his stubbly face. It was me, but it was me from a different time and place.

I was in terrified awe at the beasts flying in the sky and the ever pulsating and throbbing sun, swollen, seeming to be infected, and leaking a twilight puss over the auburn sky. I looked at him as quizzically as I could, for I knew this man was me, but still, I could not formulate words. I thought that he seemed quite calm around the flying megafauna. 'If he hadn't seen them yet, the poor bastard would see them soon enough.'[32] He stepped in closer to me and kissed me on the cheek, our stubble rubbing together as I wobbled into his arms. "Shh, buddy, relax, you'll be okay," he repeated over and over as sweat from the fear that gripped me mixed with his as I crumpled my head upon his chest. He held my chin up to his face and rubbed the top of my head like one would an understudy who's done well or a boy one looks after. His grey-toothed smile seemed like the smile of one who's seen danger and loved every minute of it. "You know, Matanza," he said, "the absolute worst part of loving someone is not the passion—in the Latin sense—but the longing; the worst part of longing is not the depression of loneliness but the love of nostalgia; the worst part of nostalgia is the lack of intimacy, the lack of

---

[32] . Paraphrased from memory: Dr. Hunter S. Thompson's opening chapter in *Fear and Loathing in Las Vegas*. The author, during this section of writing, had gone through incredible PTSD for over five years. He was self-medicating with various mixed drinks and poisonous amounts of benzodiazepam. The struggle with alienation, isolation; fits of odd and reckless behavior due to social anxiety had been ongoing for years. The concept of *being understood* is the main reason for the composition of this novel, therefore, Dr. Thompson's work felt appropriate to cite, since that passage in *Fear and Loathing in Las Vegas*, elucidated the common feelings of madness and uncontrolled hedonism that the author of this novel wished he had the bravery and honest self-enmity that Thompson so graciously elucidated in the character of Raoul Duke.

privacy, and the rights inherent to us all of self-determination and ownership, because when you love someone, you lose yourself in them forever." I tried to get my mind oriented into his cardinal point and struggled. I was finally able to stand and look him directly in the eyes. He was me for sure but one who commanded strength, yet with a deep sadness hiding in the dark brown of his dangerous eyes.

I spat on the ground and swished saliva around my mouth to remove the sticky and bitter leftovers of the memory and magic I'd smoked. "You speak of love?" I said as he smiled a reckless and happy smile. "Even in the darkest of nights here, when the wind blows, it has the warmth of Persephone's flesh. So, I think I do love her."

He laughed heartily and patted me with a broad heavy hand on the shoulder. Then returned his hands to his waist, a vision of pride and power. "You love her? For real? You? Matanza? The Mother of Tigers and the foremost murderer in Western Africa? Well, that is a first!" He laughed heartily from his belly and ran his hand across his stubbly cheeks and lips. "It's quite hot here, and dry. Shit, what we need is some whiskey gingers and lime."

"What should I call you?" I asked, still recovering from my bad trip. "I mean, you seem to be me, but a different me from a different place." He looked at me and rocked a little back and forth. "Hmm, let's see… Call me 'Alcazar.' And yes, Matanza, I am who you say I am, and I have been a part of you since both of our births." I looked at him and reached for a cigarette from my case. I opened it, and he quickly reached in and grabbed one. "Yep, sorry, my man, I could really use a smoke." We put our smokes simultaneously into our pursed lips. I lit mine with a match, and he cupped my match hand with both his large hands, as broad as the flippers on a dolphin, and stuck his face in and lit his.

"Both of our births?" I asked quizzically.

"Yes, my man, when one life ends another begins, right?" he said as he inhaled, the paper of the cigarette crackling as the cherry burned down. He let blue smoke fall out of his mouth like the wisps of an airy waterfall. "Yep, buddy, I have been here from the start. I think it was a few thousand years ago, or maybe a week ago, when you first got to the outer islands, the morning all purple and orange, the sun bright in the dawn sky. You warily removed yourself from the burden of accomplishing little in the way of work, straightened your enormous glasses upon your face, picked up a small chunk of driftwood, and put five odd-looking seashells in your pocket. I've seen it all." I had a dissatisfied urge to hear stories of my past life, since I remembered nothing. Memories are the fibers of character. I am a man without character, a passive and static vehicle.

"Tell me, Alcazar, what was my life? What can I learn from my past? What laws did I believe in? What God did I pray to? What was I to the world?"

He looked at me and smirked deviously. "The only questions your history can teach you, Matanza, Mother of Tigers, are that the strange queries that you may think the most burning will be metamorphosed before you can even answer them, only to be succeeded by others, and the singular process of your self-discovery will splinter and shiver the notions that you now use to describe your perplexity," he said seriously, albeit with smatterings of impish wit.

His answer was as perplexing and as a fathomless as what St. Lazarus might have said. "So, I am to be a storyteller and a scribe here? A keeper of records and one who deals in fables? How can I tell fables when I don't have a belief in anything but magic, much less any God?" I asked Alcazar as he sat on a rocky black outcropping, pointing at the sky with his finger and counting the flying beasts in the air.

"Well, Matanza, I would answer you by saying that a storyteller of any weight does not have to believe in God but must believe in mankind, in all of his shallow ardor. I know you have no memories or character, but I am thinking of a time when you were a boy and you would lose yourself in deep thought, deeper thought than any boy should endeavor. Long ago, when you saw your father and his friends enjoying their time together, they were all like young barbarians skylarking, childlike, and at play. You were too old for your years and never lived those happy moments later in life, how sad it was."

His answer made me misty-eyed, not for any reason but that I once had a father and wondered if he lived a joyful life and if I was a good son. "I cannot abide by the laws of this place, Alcazar; I want to know what I have been. It's a solid and throbbing suffering to not even understand what motivates me."

He looked up at me and adjusted the boonie hat high upon his head, raising his hand above his squinting eyes to shade himself from the sun.

"And what of laws here? Is there no political ethos we must follow? No rules or morality?" I said, frustrated.

"Ah... political ethics are to be answered by natural law, which alone determines what is right, good, just, and proper, and all of their alternatives. We find all of that within ourselves and our own wants and needs. If a law is unjust to you then is it just to break it?" said Alcazar as he begged me for another cigarette. I thought about how I could break the unjust rules of never knowing oneself, the politics and strange laws and magic of this place.

"You are to be a scribe and story-teller here, right? Is that the most noble of pursuits?" he asked as he spat on the ground and dipped his head low atop his crossed arms.

"I don't know what any noble pursuit may be," I said as I sat down in front of him. "I wonder what the most virtuous pursuit is. That being one that brings together all of the disciplines and philosophies, skills and gifts of an individual." I paused for a second as Alcazar looked attentively at me. "Could storytelling and rhetoric and grammar and language, could they be the most noble? Teaching?"

He pulled a small three-ounce flask out of his shirt pocket and took a swig. "Palm wine and rum," he said as he shuddered from the drink's strength. "Every pursuit that one endeavors to use to put food on a table for those who love you is noble, yet what pure craft requires every virtue and learned skill? I would have to say that politics and gamesmanship is where everything can come together. I am not by any means saying that politicians are virtuous. I am saying that a perfect politician, who has never existed, would have to be as caring and compassionate as a mother to her foal, as strong as the yews that make bows, as gifted in oratory as Apollo, as honest and wise as Socrates, and as ambitious as Alexander. However, that person will never exist, so for those spirits here with you now, they must use you as their council and keeper of secrets, judge and ambassador, storyteller and orator. You can have great power here, great power, or you can let it all go and disappear forever into the ether of endless chance and expectations."

"Endless and boundless chance, eh?" I said as I thought that leaving this place offered more mysteries than answers.

"Yep, true. If you choose to enter the epedaphic firmament with me, for instance, then there are mysteries and complexities unbounded," he said while spitting into the sand.

"Then is nothing real?" I asked as I grabbed for yet another cigarette, lighting the next one with the ember from the last.

Alcazar took another swig from his flask of palm wine and rum. "We have lost touch with the real and all its ends because we have lost touch with grace and ideas, and we have lost touch with grace and ideas because we are quite far from the purest means of reality, which is the story and the learned men and women who tell them—the truest form of art and artists[33]. That is why they want you to tell them tales and write their histories. Or you can give up any chance of atonement for your multitude of terrible sins and take a chance and leave forever," said Alcazar with a broad smile, showing chapped lips and worn-down gums. He reached into his olive drab shirt pocket and took out a small red notebook, the cover of which had written upon it "Notas." He opened it to *pagina sesenta y sies*, a

---

[33] . The Author believes that art; the expression of scholarship—emotions, hatred and love, passions and fears—using honest creativity has been destroyed by the commodifying and mass production of *"creativity for profit."* This is tied to the factory-based system of western education, the reliance of *specializations* in higher learning, not focusing on being *well read*, and ignoring critical thinking, qualitative research, and the omniscience of wisdom found through the ideas hypothesized and proven factual by historical, contemporary, and modern scholars; mathematicians, artists, philosophers, and scientists.

few pages from a bookmark made from human skin, and ran his finger down the lines until he reached one and stopped, looked up at me and smiled. "Would you like to hear something you wrote to yourself lifetimes ago in the deepest and darkest parts of Angola?" A wave of excitement came up through me and I stammered out a nervous "Yes" as he looked back down to the yellow pages and began to read.

"'What is the root of all conflict? It boils down to the omission of another's basic human needs, and when one realizes that we need so little to be happy—so small are the things that bring joy and love—then one can really lose oneself in kindness and our needs become basic and trivial. I choose not to be angered at accidents common or unavoidable; however, if you take away the things that I love, or the people that matter, then I will follow you to the ends of the Earth. If you cut off my legs and arms, I will continue looking for grace on my four bloody stumps, and if you were to slit my throat, I would utter my love in gurgled, foamy, and bubbly bloody grunts. I am not angry, and I choose grace over conflict, and the love of my friends over anger and the corrosive and heady sadness of self-imposed isolation. I have a love for people that goes deeper than any ocean, deep under the waves that rock and roll us and all the tides that break on the shore, and is stronger than every storm that blows fiercely, and the rain and wind that batter us, and those elemental forces that break even the strongest people—this is how much I love our shared humanity. I am as ardent and fervent in my unendurable compassion as time is endless and as the sun burns and bleaches our bones. I will love everyone until we all return to the Earth as fragments of splintered debris and soil.'"

Alcazar looked up at me. I had tears in my eyes and was holding back a torrent of emotion. "You were quite the odd man, Matanza. You were a man who had values and a strong compass that led you from being inordinately kind to becoming a monster through having your sensitive heart torn to bits over and over. As eloquent as your words may have been, they masked a coarse self-loathing and bitterness."

I was still holding back emotion as I ran my fingers through my soppy, moist, curly hair and licked my chapped lips. "Is there no way I can move on from those things, those moments, my past and my fears? Are there no rules or law or God who can forgive me?" I said cautiously, as if I didn't want to hear the answer.

Alcazar laughed and put two fingers to his lips, making the universal sign for smoking. I passed him another cigarette and lit it for him. He took a deep breath of it and languidly lounged back luxuriously with a satisfied, wholesome contentment. "Well, you are now part of a strange culture here, Tigermother. What is right and what is wrong, is what this given culture believes is right and wrong. It is their way of subscribing to cultural relativism. You all share your bodies with each other, you drink from the same bottles, and you have left all churches and forms of worship except those celebrating the love and forgiveness of Persephone and of the matropater that you loved in your dreams." He looked up at me and continued. "Do you think that you can find forgiveness in those things? Maybe you should run far out into the thin horizon and disappear slowly into the undulating currents of sunrise and sunset, becoming the purple hue of the dawn and dusk. Just leave, brother, leave this place: you aren't ready for or worthy of forgiveness." He paused for a second. "Take your place back up in the sky, for you are the fallen morning-star, disgraced and shunned by God."

"Doesn't forgiveness stem from love?" I asked Alcazar as he slowly put the red notebook back into his pocket. "It doesn't stem from hatred or conflict."

Alcazar fiddled with the dog tags on his chest, jingling the small round metal tabs and pulling on them. I could tell he was thinking of something. I started talking as he ran his fingers over the upside-down crucifix on his chest. "I don't know of the hatred of another due to what makes them different; this concept is alien to me. Are we not all childlike in our love for one another? I see St. Vitus—an old and brown man who jerks like a baby parrot; I see St. Lazarus—a man so foul and hircine that the phiz and tinge of his skin resemble a shaven beast's; I see The Babirusa—a genderless godhead enrobed in enormous power; I see Jolene as a collection of ocean garbage and Persephone as a nut-brown sexual deviant switch submissive whom I happen to love filially. The question is why hate another for their differences when we all bleed the same, screw the same, and love, albeit with different intentions and motivations? But it's all one and the same in the end; all love, filial, sexual, amicable, or contentious, all springs from the same roots. I don't see how in the past, or now, I am not worthy of forgiveness when I am surrounded by the love of strange things and people. And what of power? Am I not to become a powerful figure here, a knower and seer?"

Alcazar looked up at me and had the confident and dangerous look of one who is ready to get at any trouble and drink and fuck anything that moves, that animal force one sees in the tropics or in people who smell of sour sex and sweat. "I'll tell you how powerful you can be here, and then I'll give you my two cents on what you should do." He took a greenish wad of moist leaves from under his boonie cap, pushed them into his mouth, and began to chew. "Khat[34]," he said as he spat a yellow foam onto the ground. "You find yourself in the strange outer islands at a time that expands and contracts fluidly—a singular and peculiar time (or so it was and has been for you at least). These islands, slumping, rambling by an interminable and lustrous bending beach where St. Lazarus corrupts you, Persephone mends nets, St. Vitus the fishmonger fingers the rock holes for crabs and oysters, and you watch the breaking waves endlessly for the next arrival, who may come from the Indus or the Orient, lands of the tigers and lions, close-fisted baboons, cheap knock-off toys, and strong tobacco, bringing with them an even deeper magic than this place has, teaching you the knowledge of the east, and the mysticism of solitude, where they can read us the Bhagavad Gita and proclaim as Duryodhana said, 'This force of ours guarded by Bhishma is unbounded; although this force, of theirs, guarded by Bhishma, is bounded'; and you will reply as the most learned scribe on these islands, 'All those for whom I'd want to live it up are here to die,' and look the strangers in the eye when you become the wisest and say, 'I am become death, the

---

[34] The author had numerous experiences with khat on various travels throughout the northern areas of eastern Africa and some peninsular parts of the middle east. He found it quite similar to "yerba mate" with crumbled coca leaves in the gourd, as is custom in the altiplano of South America. Places such as Jujuy, any crossing of high mountain ranges, Lima, and Bolivia; as well as any travel between 3200 and 5000 meters in height, yerba mate with coca leaves is quite an important item to bring. He has never gone over the 5000-meter mark.

destroyer of worlds.'"[35] He paused for a moment and took a heavy breath. "Can you grasp how powerful you will be if you choose to stay here?" I nodded yes, as the weight of the strange words resounded within me. "If I were you, which I am, I would reject such influence and power, reject the forgiveness we don't deserve; I would reject all strange love and grace and leave this place, entering only into the galaxy where in isolation we can both find peace. There is an immense nothingness to melt into and chances as numerous as the grains of sand on this beach. There is only one choice with two outcomes, and you must choose for both of us."

My heart was beating at the bars of its cage as I slowly began to understand that this life here was a series of incredible choices yet to be made and fathomless possibilities. Alcazar had disappeared before I could respond, the rock laid bare where he sat, only the yellow spit on the ground, cigarette butts, and his boot prints remaining. Reaching back into my pocket and grabbing my small flask, I took a large sip of syrupy rum, sweet and rich as spiced buttered honey, took a heavy drag off my cigarette, finishing the entire smoke in one puff, spat into an empty tin can sounding a sharp "ping" that surprised me, looked up at the sky, counted the bumps on the

---

[35]. The author has mostly studied western philosophy, Abrahamic religious texts, Gnosticism, and Japanese bushido. This passage marks the first time he has incorporated knowledge from the Indian subcontinent. It began after researching "language and power," subsequently peaking at Russell Library in Middletown CT after researching Oppenheimer and the language of nuclear power and responsibility. The study ended with a brief but thorough reading of Hindu religious source material, and a coffee with a uniquely luminous Wesleyan undergraduate student, who was brilliantly, but nervously rambling about the geometry and shapes she admires in clouds. (Especially when travelling by rail and planes on bright sun-filled days.)

puffy and white cotton candy clouds, covered my eyes from the bright sun, and threw a seashell onto the waves, skipping it for a few yards before it disappeared under the waves. Then, I walked back towards the west where the giant flying beasts from my bad trip had all either dropped into the ocean or had their wings burned off from flying too close to the sun, and I was feeling touched with self-hatred and bitterness again.

The inferno, fear, and the fall

10

I was in a foul mood. I don't understand why one gets into negative and over-wrought emotional states, but I was feeling off, tense and strange, probably still coming off the effect of the acrid and stale paper cigar. I thought I heard cathedral bells of in the distance, or the call to prayer from an Imam. The waves shuddered against the shore like the heavy thump of a broken heart; my fists were balled up in anxiety and my arms swung, apelike, as I walked across the wet sand, leaving heavy impressions showing perfect toes. A cricket from the dune grasses creaked like a wooden floorboard in an old house, and the palm trees shook off their dates in the strong breeze. I picked up a few seashells off the beach and put them in my pocket while looking for some trouble to get into.

I thought about *kindness* on my walk towards where I thought St. Lazarus was camped. I thought about all the interactions I had had here, and the ones I didn't remember from my past births and deaths. I thought about worship and divinity. When one finds oneself alone and scared and sad, sometimes in the grand scheme of life there is someone who cares for you. Maybe one day many years ago in a lifetime far from these shores, I showed someone kindness, maybe I helped someone and didn't even realize it; but, even at my most fragile and most broken there may always have been a kindness that another being could show me that glued my brokenness into a whole. I don't know if there was however. Those must be marvelous moments to liver, and those human beings who love others are angels and spirits that heal. I should worship people in all their complexities and fractures, they are, and will be, more present than any God or gods in your life. Although, with what I have been hearing about myself, I had my doubts. I didn't know if I had ever been liked. In all honesty, I thought that I may have only been in people's lives for a moment, almost as bright and as hot as the sun, burned an impression onto another's skin, tattooing them with memories of me, and then just disappeared back into solitude and misanthropy and violence.

I felt as though I was bubbling like a boiling pot. I know that deep inside of me lies dormant a great and terrible force, a hunger for power and the longing for suffering. I knew that under the folds of my skin, deep in between my muscles and organs, there lies a desire to suffer and to leave all people who care for me, to go far and cause pain, a deviant and unhealthy fixation on anxiety and gross apathy towards kindness. I should leave this place to the spirits who dwell here and find redemption in solitary melancholy—since as an aberrant man

I am addicted to suffering and unworthy of any forgiveness and grace—and leave the storytelling for another lost specter.

I finally reached the palm-frond hut where St. Lazarus and I had spent ages together. Surrounding everything around me, and heard glaringly loud, was Mozart's Adagio and Fugue in C-minor bursting passionately through the clouds, haunting, beautiful, and terrifying. The palm logs were arranged around the fire pit where enormous sea animals lay torn open, skin on, fins on, and unscaled on spits. The coals of the old fire smoldered, auburn smoke rising from the dried palm leaves, smelling of offerings on a balmy Palm Sunday, a sunny and warm spring day where you would run into the other fair-weather Christians and sinners who find revulsion in the holy communion. I grabbed at a fire-blackened kettle and placed it on the coals to warm water for a stiff hot toddy. There, alone I stood by my fire, a witness to time, immune to death and decay, my eyes following the long curving beach, white sanded and shiny in the opalescent dawn, immense seagulls dipping into the ocean with great splashes with the sonic booms of fighter jets, my black kettle boiling over, licked by the tips of the flames, sounding like the rumble of a panzer tank, and the dragonflies and sparrows beating their wings with the chop-chop-chop of an apache helicopter, and the waves, thunderous like millions of bombs going off at a steady and rolling beat in concert. "I am the only one able to leave this place," I said to myself under my breath.

Near my foot I saw the bottle that once contained Aphrodite's rotten heart and I emptied its contents out onto the coals. Immediately there was a conflagration that singed my eyebrows off and stuck red-hot embers to my skin. The enormity of the blast was indescribable, but it felt wonderful to set things off, maybe like summer memories of catching bright fireflies and playing with friends in the woods, memories I don't have. It felt good to burn things. I stepped into the ring of logs that surrounded the giant bonfire, and flames were reaching so uncontrollably high into the sky that I could imagine them burning the bottom of the clouds, the smoke billowing like a blue and dark brown geyser of ash and sparks that popped and snapped like tiny firecrackers and sparklers soaked in bacon grease and nitroglycerin. The seabirds that were unfortunate enough to fly too near the fire burst into flames and dropped into the ocean like gasoline-soaked rags and Greek fire thrown from a ship. Some birds landed on the far-away beach where they exploded on impact, trailing streams of yellow fire like napalm and igniting the sea grasses until the whole place was ablaze and smelled like a wet hay-fire in a wooden barn. The roasting sea fishes—or ocean monsters—that hung over the fire were open mouthed and big eyed as their oily skin bubbled and spat out juice.

I put a cigarette in my mouth, lit it, inhaled, picked up a couple of charred crickets, ate them while kicking a jagged tin can and cutting a small but deep gash on my toe, and took a swig of rum and water. It felt good to light things on fire.

"Dance with me," I heard in a familiar sharp metallic voice.

"Jolene?" I said as I looked down onto the ground and saw a burlap sack. I opened it and inside was the plastic milk crate, chalkboard, opinel knife, and rubber band ball. "How am I to dance with you if you are just a collection of ocean garbage?" I asked, somewhat vexed.

I heard a loud hissing like a leaky pressure cooker and her monotone voice belted out, "Pick up the bag and just dance around. You've never danced with a woman before?" I laughed at my circumstance and picked up the burlap sack that was soaked through with sea water and heavy.

"Wait!" I said, "What about the music?"

I heard her laugh like fingers being scratched down a chalkboard. "Reach back into my bag and find my radio." I stuck my hand in and picked up a big boxy plastic cube with rounded edges. "It's a sky-blue and gold Westinghouse little jewel portable radio given to me by my love, the wind," she said. "It only plays 'Desperados Under the Eaves' by Warren Zevon on a continuous loop, but it's okay, we can get a few dances from that." Mozart's Adagio and Fugue continued blaring ominously. The Westinghouse radio struggled to pump out the Zevon song, its small-coned speaker throbbed weakly, like a new-born baby's heart: The broken heart of a baby that has never been held.

I danced with Jolene for what seemed like days until over the horizon I saw St. Lazarus, Persephone, and St. Vitus appear and walk towards the fire pit with the blazing orange and gold inferno behind them, in front of them, and all around them, unfazed by the smoke, proud and powerful, almost inebriating me with their familiar passions, sharing a large bottle of alcohol, all statues smoking and drinking, wrapped in burlap—witnesses chiseled from marble by the blowing breezes and eroded by sand on the beach, where they stood with no escape. I, however, could leave. I could do it. They were here one thousand years for every drop of rain that has fallen or will fall to Earth. I stopped dancing.

St. Lazarus carried the guitar of the dead by the neck, the body resting atop his shoulder, St. Vitus was constantly swigging his unending Turbo King beer, and Persephone was flaunting a large sea glass bottle of what seemed to be distilled spirits from some strange island plant. They were laughing and stumbling into each other.

"Matanza!" yelled St. Lazarus. "You forgot the guitar of the dead, my man, now it's time for the fire skull dance and all kinds of sinning, my little friend." His yellow grin and wobbly body shivered at the strength of Persephone's booze when he took a sip. I wasn't too intimidated by him anymore. He wasn't all that commanding; he was impressively ambidextrous in his mediocrity, always achieving a fabulous sub-parity without much effort and pretension. Kind of like a know-it-all and braggadocious artist too high and entitled from his lackluster talent.

St. Vitus, jerking his face and shaking, looked up at me. "You look worried, Mother of Tigers. What ails you?" I looked back at them with a deadpan expression. "I met myself, or what I used to be. We talked for a bit." They all looked at each other with troubled expressions on their faces.

Persephone broke the silence nervously. "Oh, don't worry about that or Alcazar or any of those matters. Hey! It seems like it's been an age—let's drink and sing songs… let's all be friends."

St. Vitus chimed in right after. "When your contest with insensibility and lethargy has been wrestled with and conquered, when these islands, here, are all encompassing night and agoraphobic silence, when all the strong-smelling perfumed smoke and sweet sticky rum takes on a whole new meaning and pages upon pages of old yellowing paper with all of our stories scratched upon them are thrown across the beach by your feet, you having written them, then, and only then, it may seem as if all of the silly things you worry about and that meander through your odd mind disappear and give way to a crystal clear and glorious lucidity." I found his words hard to believe. My heart was becoming heavy with self-loathing and poignant revulsion. After hearing that I am, and was, reprehensible, and will always be, I wanted less and less to do with spirits and magic. I walked slowly to a log near the fire and sat quietly as I didn't want to drink or talk. Jolene would occasionally join in on the banter with the spirits, hissing and grinding out drinking songs. I thought about leaving, and the choice was becoming easier to make.

St. Lazarus was plucking the string of the guitar of the dead aimlessly, and all the other ghosts and gods swayed their heads. "Matanza! I know what troubles you," he said, slurring his words and dangling his dog-like broad tongue through his teeth. "It is said that in the beginning there was a great void, a starless and dark empty space, and a cauldron of fire under it all, slowly expanding and contracting gases and proteins, and from that all-encompassing fire were born the stars and galaxies, and they in turn birthed the rivers and oceans, and then the auroras from the multitude of suns burned the giants and spirits into forms from the rocky bones of moons and planets, and from that stew of cosmic accidents came mankind and his beliefs. You, Matanza, were coagulated into a placenta-covered bastard child of the stars where at your birth you were licked clean like a baby calf by tigers, elephants, and the wild dogs of the jungles. You are the unwanted sire and trash of the cosmos. Alcazar said the same." I lit a cigarette. He was right.

Persephone was sneaking glances at me as she joked and laughed with the others, then sat next to me and rested her head on my shoulder. As she stared into the fire, she whispered, "Over the multitude of eons I have seen failures of all kinds and types. I have seen men lose fortunes on a game of pitch and toss and regain them through enterprise. I have seen men spoken foul of by enemies and those who covet their women, wine, and wisdom, yet they disregarded all lies told of them and achieved greatness. I have seen the cupulas of all great religious temples destroyed and razed into ashes of marble and mortar, yet men and women seem to always build other ideologies from their ashes—always failing and causing conflict, one reincarnation after another of pompous piety and lies. You see, men and women are tribal; they want to belong to a collection of people and ideas, nations, states, based on corrupt religions and faltering society built on ancient ideas, once pragmatic, now old and decayed. You, however, don't care for the thought of others; you are alone in your silence and suffering as you gently take in all you see. As a man, you, when troubled, turned to violence and caused great harm; as the fallen angel, you inspired men into all cruelties. Now at the time of your redemption and ascent into power, you vacillate and wonder if solitude among the stars and moons would be befitting your past crimes. You cannot remove the silence and solitude from men of your nature; it lasts long after their deaths. You do what you must do—I'll be your friend regardless. I care for you."

St. Lazarus grabbed me and stood me up, almost throwing me across the fire where he put his arm around me and shoved a bottle of booze in my face. "Drink this, my little friend. Don't trouble yourself, tell us stories, write our stories." Persephone, St. Vitus, and Jolene all raised their voices in a chorus. "Tell us our tales, tell us stories, c'mon!" St. Lazarus whispered in my ear. "Look at Persephone right now; she's ready and willing, and tonight is the night of the fire skull dance. Throw away all morality; it's all relative," he said as he smiled a grey toothy grin.

I looked up at him, quite vexed. "I argue that for morality to be more than merely relative and contingent, it must be guaranteed by a supreme being," I said in nervous anger. St. Lazarus laughed a potbellied squeal and pointed at Persephone.

"Supreme being!" He laughed again. "We need protection from God! Persephone is theodicy embodied, she is our defense from God's goodness and omnipotence in view of any apparent evil. She destroys us unrepentantly and reconstitutes us nightly with her forgiveness and grace. Just let yourself be forgiven, Tigermother." For the first time on these islands, I saw a look of concern on St. Lazarus' face.

I could see Persephone stealing glances longingly and nervously up at my face. She looked concerned. St. Vitus still shivered as he constantly drank from his giant bottle of Turbo King. Jolene hissed through the din of nervous laughter and strange music. "There are only a few men who have come close to being you; one man gave everything away to climb the highest peaks in the Tibetan altiplano, only to perish, and his fossilized Denisovan jawbone was found eons later by a crippled monk in a cave; he found true wisdom. Another man tried to dig a hole so deep that he was able to puncture the ceiling of Tartarus and fell deep into an everlasting free-fall whereas he tumbled deeper and deeper he learned more and more, and it is said that he sprang through the other side of the heavens and is the keeper of a well of water where the Norse gods drink their wisdom. And finally, there is you—the man who either becomes the teller of fables and all-powerful legends or chooses to melt back into the starry night from whence he came," said Jolene in between gasps and robotic whispers.

I took a swig of the hard alcohol and felt it burn all the way down my throat into my gut. "All right, guys. I'll tell you a story." A look of absolute joy came over their faces, and I drank some more of the syrupy booze. "Have you heard the story of how a man saw Artemis nude bathing in a river and she turned him into a stag and hunted him down? She was a true stoic, never given to the softer passions or love; however, one day a young shepherd in the Macedonian foothills fell in love with the moon. He felt at home, mostly at night alone in solitude, as he guarded his flock from the wolves and the beasts of the mountain ranges. Artemis saw how devoted he was to her as she shone down brightly in the dark reek of the night sky, and deep inside of her silvery, blue, and cold heart she watched the young man every night and saw how devoted he was to the herds he protected, how he battled the wild dogs and thieves and rustlers to the death, bravely with his staff and knife, how he helped the defenseless small animals, once rearing a baby hummingbird with sweet water and nectar from the flowers of his fields, and mended the wings of a baby sparrow near death, and how he befriended the crows and the hawks high in the sky. Artemis never told the other gods of this poor, kind young man. She watched him nightly as he found peace and wisdom among the craggy rocks of the highland meadows.

Slowly, as time went on and on, the man grew older, always alone, caring for the beasts in his fields, until many years later, after a solitary life, he passed on into twilight alone at an old age, his body and bones becoming earth and dust, the wolves consumed his thick dried skin, and the vultures picked him clean. A single bush of mountain flowers grew from the rotten rags of his death cloak. It is said that one day when he was young, on his first day of understanding his terrible aloneness, Artemis flew down from her nightly perch to give the man a kiss but chose not to, only to brush her hand against his cheek as he slept; really nobody knows if she ever did or not. But the day that marked the end of this unknown man's life was the day that Artemis lost all hope in love. She suffered quietly and dedicated her time to the hunt and to nature, always with the face of the poor young man with curly hair and a kind and gentle heart in her mind's eye. It is further claimed that she carved the man's smile onto the moon where all could see it. But legends are legends, lies are lies, gods are false, truth gets lost through the ages, and nobody knows the messages anymore. Nobody speaks the language of love, and the bravery of loving another is lost in the mire of false words and cowardice. It's better to ossify one's heart, better to push love far from you, better to cause others the feelings of longing and loss, and better to revel in that aloneness that only one can cause themselves to feel."

I finished my story and sat down on a log with the wind pushing sharply at my back and making me feel at home with my decision. St. Lazarus grabbed the guitar of the dead and swept his gnarled and arthritic fingers across the nylon strings, his voice becoming deep and sonorous as he played a criollo chacarera and sang out "adentro!" as he burst into the song. St. Vitus and Persephone joined in with choruses and harmonies, the mellifluous melodies echoing throughout the caverns and rocky outcroppings. St. Lazarus' fingers, jarred with the chords and arpeggios and double stops, were plucked hard with his long yellow fingernails as he sang about love and life, asados, and humble people from humble places, lives and loves lost, games played, fortunes made and squandered. In the short and powerful song, St. Vitus, Persephone, and St. Lazarus shed tears and laughed together. They all took deep swigs of rum and water as I smoked cigarette after cigarette. St. Vitus grabbed a calf leather-skinned bombo and beat out a rhythm; Persephone danced around the fire, seducing us all, playing imaginary castanets and paper fans, the smell of brine and bodies, hung salty and thick in the air. St. Vitus and St. Lazarus pecked at Persephone's shorts as she danced with their old, gnarled, and arthritic fingers; sometimes grazing her breasts, or pinching her bottom and hard nipples, clawing ravenously like sharp taloned vultures; nipping at her like curious bloodhounds and starving rats. She pulled a chain from her pocket and wrapped it around her neck, and St. Vitus led her around the fire like a dog on all fours and stuck his fingers inside of her, and that was when the orgy began.

Mozart's Adagio and Fugue in C-minor began to be heard played backwards; the second movement came into the sky like a lightning bolt cracking through the clouds backwards. It was not frightening. It was welcome. "Mozart wrote his works as commissions to God and the church, to celebrate men and to celebrate God. It should make sense that I am calmed and feel wholeness when it is played in reverse." I walked far away with the sound of flesh beating upon wet flesh behind the horizon—the inferno raging around us all—out into the ocean as far as my feet could reach, into the darkest of oblivions, and took my final resting place among the galaxies, for I realized that I had always been a fallen star.

Adagio

The Letter to the Lost

The Mythos of Matanza

11

I find myself at your stone, where you have been laid to rest. I must say sir, that it has been neglected, for there are weeds, dandelions, high grasses that have been browned in the Connecticut summer sun—A rodent of some kind has chipped away at the bottom of your memorial, which has been made from plain brownstone: A rat is gnawing on your bones, chipped teeth, and leathery skin—Cigarette butts have left small, round and pocked craters of charred and blackened weeds; No candles ever lit, nor flowers ever placed at your feet, no visitors—besides vagrants—have graced you, or will; but I must be honest and say that it is not a melancholic place. You are resting near Gold and Main St, in Hartford. One can hear the rattle of busted up, junked Japanese cars float by, the open exhaust of once luxurious rusting Cadillacs in a dying city. It appears that this place, this city, is at rest as well, its proud history has been gerrymandered and enveloped into a noisy haze, that ever-present death of industry and pride—the buildings have become monuments themselves, to that singular and definite American avarice and an empire in decline[36].

However, I've heard conversations in four languages while visiting you. It is as though we are of one human culture, in an experiment that has gentrified and localized our differences. As people, I fear that we still are not ready for homogeneity, we still all retain divisions, constructed by those in power— tribal, ethnic, religious, political—idealized and constantly reinforced by others who wish and will it through perverse narratives, and simple people who cannot forgive the pains of eons and centuries. I will leave you, dear brother, with the findings and smattering of philosophies I was able to smuggle back from my many lifetimes on the outermost islands; the personal words of Matanza "The Tigermother;" the ideas that should never have been recorded or crystallized in any form, except those of fever dreams, passing nightmares, and anxieties.

Brother, I am to die with the knowledge you sought and fought for, the secrets you left unlearned and undiscovered: the way time has proven us both right, that we are only here to rust into husks as hairy and coarse as coconut matting, to be trampled, to become dirty and worn; to make life unpleasant for our loved ones, friends, strangers, and those most imperious fools who choose to love others, instead of embracing the numbness of knowledge, and the drug of apathy due to others' ignorance.

---

[36] We are dying, countries are dying, the world is dying. Please, please, please, let us find a way to come together as brothers and sisters. Can we all sit and talk, please? Pass me the talking stick, I will start the talk—with confidence and respect if nobody else will. I will pass to you, and you to another, then they will give the stick to their opposites.

(And with only the greatest happiness at your solitary, lonely, and suffered death—as well as mine, that I am endeavoring to undertake with a liter of bleach, a syringe, and a 6-hour loop of Victorian pornographic silent films at the Goodwin Hotel—anxious to relish each labored breath and dizzying pressure drop with grand enthusiasm—hoping to culminate my story both during a climax of pain and one of throbbing orgasm).

. . . .

-Captain Sota-

Findings on "Matanza": A Requiem for Thomas Congress
"Smaller Print"

A few years after men took their first steps onto the great and sandy surface of the moon—which smelled like asphalt and freshly fired gunpowder—and some time before the Challenger burst open in the sky, leaving puffy white trails of smoke and vapor that left the greasy residue of human remains and subcutaneous fat gelled to the sides of the space craft's porcelain heat tiles, like lumps of margarine unevenly spread onto a pan—there lived a man of no consequence to anything important that has ever happened or most likely ever will happen. He was a collector of small things. Things like bottle caps, cigarette butts, and bits of thread that he found tied to trees and bushes (only in the springtime, though, he wouldn't take string that he found in any other season.) He never loved anyone, nor could he understand nor notice the complexities of those feelings if he ever had the luck to feel them. However, he did suffer an enormous amount of pain in his life. He had the strange quality of being able to ignore any good or love that ever graced his life. Yet he felt and writhed, purposely, under the unendurable trauma of solitude and longing. He was aastone-cold, brown-eyed, curly-haired killer. His name was Matanza.

It is said in *Nichomachean Ethics* that politics is the one discipline that brings together all the arts and sciences holistically. Then, one must ask him or herself why do the most insidious and perfunctory sophists gravitate to it? If it is the most complete human endeavor, then we must all be ridiculous as people since polity is a collective of the foulest and simplest of human beings. The study of the physical sciences and mathematics, medicine, and even metallurgy has practical application in the finishing polish of the gears and machinery that ever grind away and power society under some strange and ever-self-motored mechanism. Politics, however, seems to move at a pace that is deliberate in relation to the stupidity of its adherents. Slowly, at a crawl, sometimes backwards, more like a sine wave with peaks and drops, and at times even stopping like a faulty quartz in a cheap watch.

Matanza created his own profession, on levels much obscener, more morally corrupted and debasing of pure human nature than the pursuit of politics. He was the first specialist in "the omniscience of the profane," as he was once quoted in an El Salvadorian newspaper, during his time contracted by leftist guerrillas to murder indiscriminately during the revolution in the 1980s. He called himself "the world's first professional sociopathic and profoundly amoral man of leisure."

During my journey to the three happy isles, I was told about Matanza through the correspondence of a wise Bolivian doctor and tribal medicine man who specialized in the counseling of men and women who had suffered incredible sexual traumas and emotional abuse—using alkaloids found in strange plants, dried fig leaves, and a concoction that was purified from tree frog venom mixed with the tears of a dying man. He cautioned me on our first meeting, before I became his caretaker, that Matanza had psychopathically seduced two Oxford-trained psychiatrists; one a blemish-faced, red-headed, and chubby 37-year-old manic depressive closeted Jew who hated her father, the other an older, skinny and frail, grey-haired 82-year-old Irish shrink, who suffered intense self-loathing for his Friday and Saturday night submissive sexual gluttony where he would indulge in all manner of humiliations and perversions that would lead him to 5-hour-long Sunday afternoon confessions with an alcoholic Catholic priest who called himself "Facundo Ceres," although he was really "Carlos Moya," the famed gaucho and train robber of the late 19th century. Some say Moya had a hand in taking out Cassidy and the Sundance Kid. I never found out. The Irishman's name was Murphy if I recall correctly.

Matanza seduced men and women only to the point at which they were completely drawn into the sexual encounter itself; never did he ever follow through, but only received pleasure from breaking their spirits and incredible minds with intention. He never touched these men and women, just influenced them enough to agree to things that they would never endeavor in any healthy moment of passion; he was only about seeing them break. When they did, he left, gone again, far away, to places where nobody would ever give a second thought or look for him. He once made a 16-year-old girl who ran a kiosk in Mendoza, from the noble roots of a good but poor family, steal a jar of spare change from her dying father's bureau, what only amounted to pennies and nickels that would help him live longer to see her grow up well. He had saved those few copper bits through back-breaking labor, only moved by the love of his family and the pure pride he felt for his young daughter.

He died ashamed of his child on a bright and breezy Tuesday afternoon—Jorge Cafrune's "Balderrama" was playing on a crackly tube radio. Before he passed into oblivion cursing her name through the pain of wheezy and bloody coughs, he banished her far into the mountains of Cuyo with his last words, dripping with loathing and soaked with vile bitterness and heartbreak. There she lived a suffering life of grief, unfilled memories of a happiness that never materialized, and moments of terrifying and gripping regret that peaked into days and months punctuated by the torture of sadness. Matanza put a few of those copper coins on his watch chain and would rub his fingers on them every hour or so, compulsively, as a constant reminder of how, through the poor girl's grief and salty tears from her father's death, her poor choices and her nightmares and regrets, he was personally able to live a happier, richer, and fuller life.

I have appended the last letter Matanza left in my possession, in his own handwriting, and his own language. After my translation, the letter goes as follows:

The Second Letter of Matanza
"Smaller Print"

"The Tigermother"
Address not registered
Wavemaker and Rainmaker
Laid to rest in either the Eastern or Western Ocean

Homo Sapiens
Local Group: "Orion Arm"
$2/3^{rd}$ right of the Center
Galaxy: "Milky Way"
3rd interstellar body orbiting "Sol"

Allow me to illuminate the stanzas and songs I wish you all to help me tackle in a poetic fashion and sing as human memory and saga. I feel that the gift of finding meaning and beauty in the laconic and passionate craft of poetry is honestly beyond my scope of expression. I once expressed to you all that poetry and lyricism is the hardest and most challenging form of writing. One must crystallize the minutia of our experiences into small fragments and rhythmic phrases with great meaning. I am asking, wholeheartedly, that the words you help "us" craft, be of a meaning superior to any musical theme, counterpoint, or composition that I ever endeavor. I wish to accompany these X concepts with music, composed on tortoise shell lyres, gut string bucket basses, and flutes from hollowed out femurs. I will attempt to elucidate these with brevity in mind. Please advise and think deeply; intellectualize your emotions and become computers: overthink so as not to fall into caring or the finite mistake of love. (Love is not boundless).

Sincerely,
Matanza: "The end of the night sky"

The Ten Stanzas of Matanza

Poetry of the Awful Experience: yet to be written by "us,"
humanity in concert, (the Collective, the Dead)

I

I wish to explore the concept of legacy. I would like to apologize to those I have harmed. I would like to wish those who attempted to love me only the best, since their endeavor ended falling onto bruised ears that are conversant in only the language of self-loathing and pure melancholic pity—in the sense of esteem—and a deviant and masochistic addiction to emotional pain. I would like to ask forgiveness to whatever God or Gods there may be, if any exist, and express the fact, to him or her or them, that I have gone unheard and look forward to meeting them soon to express in person—or through the ounces and evaporated droplets of anima that escape me when I dissolve into corruption—that I am within my rights to break their jaw, or tear their limbs off. I wish to communicate my deafness to those who offered compassion, and I wish to frame it in the sense of pure longing. I would like to speak of one love that has mattered, and the way we tore at each other, and the way she tried endlessly to be kind with me, and how I buried my pain and unforgiving nature in the dark places on Earth. How I repented by suffering alongside people who were liminal in society; how I lived and still live on the finest of lines, eschewing human mores and proper laws, those of man and

God; instead embracing the utter romance of chaotic danger and resentment. I purged her from my memory through suffering, in some ways flagellating my haunches and heart, all for a Christ hard of hearing and a troubled woman.

II

I would like to speak on the rights of the American, and the world-wide worker. I would like to express the concepts of how the gold of the bourgeoisie is tainted and stained with the blood of those who work the land, mines, fields, those who live honestly, albeit misguided by charlatans. How the working poor find joy in the small parts of family. How the working class has been buried in collapsing coal chutes, how the farmers' grains are rotting in silos to price gouge, how honest work is looked down upon, and how those people who form the spine of America from the Rocky Mountains to the Ohio River and to the forested hills of the Shenandoah are misrepresented and their bodies are being used to shore up the foundation of a declining empire. How no man or woman should spit blood to put food on the table. How their lives go forgotten after they leave us, and how the nameless men and women who built our country are treated as figures of pity and contempt, instead of being invested in and communities built around them.

III

I want a piece about losing myself in alcohol and painkillers. I want to explore the numbness and the seeking of danger to live in those liminal edges that I find myself most at home in. I want to speak on the romance of longing, of distance and drugs, the use of extreme violence due to my perverse sense of justice, and how I can disregard the violence and antipathy I cause in those I fight, which have been many, and at much loss, since I have never won a proper fight fairly. I want to express how I have turned into a mythos, how I became a caricature of my own design. How I somehow coagulated into a mass of a broken man, one who loses himself in tragedy and adventure. I am a solitary and insular man, as you are now aware, who bites at his rancor and cannot accept kindness without that nagging voice of bitterness or paranoia of ulterior motives. Express in some way who I am, for never being understood in my wholeness has left me shivered into pieces, like a whiskey-filled tumbler, in a dark smoke-filled room, thrown onto a hardwood floor.

IV

I want a proper ode to a complicated woman. Someone whose incredible kindness was torn apart by exploitation. How I fell in love with her small hands and smile, and how she worked with dignity, until drug addled and bruised—raspberry-blotted purple and blue-pricked veins, numb gums, and cold shots into her knuckles—she drowned in suffering, unable to forgive herself for the drive of needing to feel perverse and complex pain to atone. How she has survived by selling herself, and how she cries every night alone at a bar, always friendless, connecting only with the tigers that buy her blowjobs for cocaine. How my thoughts drift back into her, how distance and danger is how I forget her. How I am much more complicated than she is, a worse person, a man who has caused more pain to others, and yet find myself in judgment of her and hold in my heart the unjust premise that I have always been a better person than she.

V

I would like a series of loose compositions that can dreamily explore the warm embrace of benzodiazepam, how depressed and labored the breathing becomes after mixing a multitude of the green pills with a quart of whisky, how speech is slurred, how the mind shines a dull opaque and confusing hue, how sleep comes and goes through fantasies and colors, how stories and dreams and what is real become mixed into an ever-darkening pallet—smeared and smokey—with the occasional punctuation of colors through the haze, how drugs numb the fear of love and the need for it. Never forgetting that jarring and reviving sting of a Camel or Lucky Strike burning down into one's finger during the orgasmic deadness of wheezy gasps for air in the silence and quiet one finds in somber and dull auto-asphyxiated sleep.

VI

I would like a piece that celebrates the body of a woman or man. How that first moment of holding their hips has a magic that is unforgettable. How mutual seduction opens people up to complexities that humanity still isn't ready for, and may never be, since famously and throughout history men and women have cannibalized each other, philosophized and weaponized sex into affairs of power and influence, for control and oppression and exploitation, rarely framing it for that wrenchingly beautifully tart, lemony, and ocean-salt mineral taste a partner leaves in your mouth, and for the trust of bonds being solidified through physical pressure and the gravitas of openly imbibing the thoughts and vulnerabilities of the nude human form, and the spirit and mind behind it. How people have mystery and depth that they hold onto just long enough to feel the pain of disappointment in love. Often clamming up after recurring wounds, failures that slowly eat away at that once-readily open heart, sometimes balling up and carbonizing into a diamond-like, shame-triggering sexual deviance that one hopes hides the pangs of compassion, that kink that one uses to atone for being silly enough to even have loved in the first place.

VII

Death. I would like to explore the dead and dying deities, the absence of God and love and the looming oblivion that we all pack away deep into our marrow. The idea that there is nothing more valuable than glory. That the pursuit of glory is worth dying for, that the "love of your life" is what you *erroneously* go to war for, the idea that one should accept death as a reality that is not special or noteworthy. That people forget you, that photographs fade, and that you will be lost in the multitude of millions of bones beneath our feet without making a difference. That the special "one," that woman or man who created a life with you, will move on, and that your children's voices will utter your name less and less. The only worse thing than that is knowing that you left personal glory behind on the table for another to exploit. Finally, that last tiny ember that you left on Earth, that one thing that will spontaneously burst into flames, indirectly leaving its mark in every future generation, manifesting centuries into the distant and immeasurable sine wave of time, will be how much you fucked up your kids.

VIII

The incommunicable experience of witnessing war deep in the swarming jungle, where the green of the equator's bounty concealed gray and chartreuse bones, thick with bits of hanging black-skinned flesh shrouded in rotting cotton olive drab fatigues, bodies that become leaky purple balloons, popping into a gelatinous mass that quickly dissolves into the red loamy soil. Dodging AK47 rounds while occasional .50-caliber DShK rounds rip chunks off banana tree trunks behind you. Those old willie jeeps running on tinpot lawnmower engines, motorcycle taxis, drinking Turbo King beers with lunatics, pirates, mercenaries, and racists. Getting a kiss from a confused and homesick Swiss nun, during that one precious moment of vulnerability where she allowed a gently placed hand on her neck and breast in a shared moment of unique passion. After which one can find oneself wholeheartedly enjoying her smile, tinged with a rosy-cheeked sadness, and the embrace of a deep regret, as she realized that she had just broken her sacrosanct covenant with God—hoping she felt my thrill. A just God would never let human beings commit the cruelties I witnessed.

IX

The exploitation of the poor, the hypocrisy of the helpers, the fiat politics of kindness and absolute truth in pure meanness, the bureaucracy that ties up the decent and misguided intentions of kind people, who are drowned out in the vocal and base madness of the mob. That unheralded greatness that humans rarely achieve and the invisibility that the poor live in, unable to even dream. The voices that go unheard, the talents that never become real or are ever nurtured. The waste of lives spent on the trivial and small. That American lie of upward mobility and the circle of poverty, misguided education, and the manufactured pursuit of excess that is so intoxicating and inescapable.

X

Alcohol-fueled nights of Pall Mall filterless cigarettes, fingerpicking Andean melodies, Jorge Cafrune and Atahualpa Yupanqui concerts, worshipping the "Pacha Mama" and pretty women, dancing until the sun rises, ladies who pass in the night, but only after leaving incredible moments that last in memories forever, until one passes onto whatever other plane exists, if any. Living life to the brim, laughing, whiskey highballs, kissing a girl with a nice smile. The women who mean a lot for a little and leave. The love of walking barefoot in the grass, stars shining brightly and large blood moons. Howling at expansive milky night skies, sleeping in the forest, and the beauty of finding grace in introspection and solitude.

-fin-

Le début d'une nouvelle aube

CPSIA information can be obtained
at www.ICGtesting.com
Printed in the USA
BVHW030156081021
618510BV00006B/198